VALENTINE

VALENTINE

A NOVEL

Lucius Shepard

FOUR WALLS EIGHT WINDOWS

NEW YORK / LONDON

2002

Published in the United States by
Four Walls Eight Windows
39 West 14th Street, room 503
New York, NY 10011
http://www.4W8W.com

Library of Congress Cataloging-in-Publication Data:
    Shepard, Lucius.
    Valentine : a novel / Lucius Shepard.

    p.   cm.
    ISBN 1-56858-215-3
    1. First loves—Fiction. 2. Journalists—Fiction. 3. Hurricanes—Fiction.
    4. Florida—Fiction. I. Title.

    PS3569.H3939 V35 2002
    813'.54—dc21

                        2001040434

Text design and composition by Ink, Inc., New York.
Printed in the United States

10   9   8   7   6   5   4   3   2   1

For You

VALENTINE

THERE ARE COUNTRIES THAT EXIST only for a matter of days, sometimes only for hours, not lasting long enough to be named or even recognized for what they are by their temporary citizenry. Often they are created by fog banks, hurricanes, blizzards, by any force of nature with the power to isolate; on other occasions they are brought into being by incidences of cosmic weather, shifts in dimensionality and the like, events to which many of us in our stubborn rationality refuse to subscribe. Whatever the character of their borders, for the duration of their existence these countries are governed by their own peculiar laws, which we are persuaded to accept as logical and right, no matter how illogical and wrong they might strike us were we back in the country of our birth; and because we accept them, because we yield ourselves up to their remarkable processes, the unremarkable stuff of our lives may be transformed forever.

I am writing this during the week immediately preceding Valentine's Day, nearly three months after you and I met in just such a country, an encounter that you may not remember. Though I did not consciously choose the moment to write, I can't deny that the day is appropriate to the task—a day when the confusions of love are cast aside and the essence of that emotion is expressed simply by means of heartfelt gifts and heart-shaped cards. What I have to say does not in itself constitute a simple expression, being a detailed record of our time together and referencing other times when we have shared the same latitude and longitude. But perhaps the simplicity of the form, a letter, will convey the simplicity of the feelings that inspire it and so find its way to your heart.

Toward the end of last November, I was on assignment for *Natural History*, driving down the west coast of Florida, some eighty miles north of Fort Myers, when a hurricane alert was announced on the radio. It was extremely late in the year for a hurricane, and I saw no sign of impending bad weather; but to be on the safe side I stopped at the next town I came to and checked into the Shangri La Hotel: a rambling structure with wooden shutters, a screened verandah, and weathered once-white boards that had likely experienced its heyday as a secret mystical kingdom back in the 1930s, and had managed to survive into the new century by catering to the elderly and the infirm. I stowed my bag in a room on the second floor, a humid claustrophobic space with cheap production line furniture and ocher walls decorated by two tropical landscapes notable for the artist's poor control of perspective. A dead palmetto bug floated in the toilet. The room would have been a terrific place in which to pitch a self-pitying drunk. Since I hadn't reached that stage of depression, I had no wish to stay there any longer than necessary. After I washed up, I went for a walk along the beach.

The town to which the hotel belonged was Piersall, named for Jeremy Gaylord Piersall, an early settler memorialized by a plaque in front of a police station the size of a Burger King. Bungalow-style houses tucked in among the palms. A boardwalk lined with arcades, souvenir shops, and rides, most of them shut down. Three blocks of business district—one-story buildings of concrete block containing a predictable assortment of drugstores, realtor's offices, beachwear shops, and lawyer's nests. A gentle surf rolled in from the Gulf, and the sky had lowered, sealing the town off from the rest of the world; yet there was no accompanying rain and no wind. It was as if an enormous hand had set a pewter cup down over the place, the way a child might imprison an insect that has attracted his attention. The air was clear where I walked, but beyond the break lay a barrier of mist, and when I turned inland I discovered that the highway had in effect been sheared away by a fog bank some twenty feet past the city limits. I'd never encountered a fog with such distinct boundaries. Two steps in, and I couldn't see my feet.

Back at the hotel I broke out my laptop, hoping to get some work done, but I began to feel out of sorts and wondered if I might not be coming down with a cold. I was giving thought to hunting up a drugstore when I heard footsteps in the corridor. I cracked the door to discover who else had been rash enough to check into the Shangri La. Just passing my room was a tall brunette woman with long legs and a serene gait. My angle was poor—I only glimpsed a partial profile.

But I knew it was you. As I shut my door I heard the door to the adjoining room open. A surge of adrenaline made my fingers tremble. What were the odds against a coincidence of this order? That eleven years after you left me and returned to your marriage, six years after our final meeting, we would wind up in the same hick town, in adjoining rooms at the same hotel?

"Jesus!" I said, and sank into a chair. I was dizzy; I could feel a rapid pulse in my neck. A couple of spins later I said again, more reverentially, "Jesus," and got to my feet. If I had seen a tiger or a burning man, I couldn't have been more dumbfounded.

Maybe, I thought, it wasn't you.

Then I could have sworn I felt you moving about on the other side of the wall. I dropped back into the chair. Nobody else but you activated my dog senses.

For a considerable time I was unable to think, overwhelmed by what had happened. I imagined the two of us glowing like two fireflies in caves set side-by-side, each believing themselves alone, but confused by an electric sense of one another. I decided to find a different hotel, motivated more by a fear of disharmony than by any notion of moral correctness. But instead I sat there replaying scenes from our serial affair. Our first night in Madison. Living together in New York. The break-up. Epistolary interludes and telephone calls. Passionate reunions. Once I figured out I wasn't going to leave, I went into the hall. I grew light-headed again, and I braced my palm against your door to steady myself. No more than half an hour had elapsed since you walked past, and I was already a wreck. I pulled myself together, knocked and stood listening to your footsteps. When you saw me, your expression of pleasant inquiry flattened out. I couldn't tell whether you were angry or alarmed, but I could tell joy wasn't part of the mix.

"What are you *doing* here?" you asked.

"Six billion people," I said. "We were bound to run into one another."

I realized you must be in shock. Whereas I'd had time to get accustomed to the idea of seeing you again, you were in the initial stages. "I'm hiding out from the hurricane," I told you.

"Me, too," you said.

The moment stretched. Grew bloated. Swelled to bursting. I was on the verge of throwing in the towel when you drew me into a sisterly hug and invited me in. The paintings on your walls were seascapes by, apparently, the same myopic artist whose work infested my room.

"I almost didn't recognize you," you said, closing the door.

"Right...the beard." I sat in a chair by the window. "It hides the gunshot wound."

You offered a frosty laugh and perched on the foot of the bed. A silence shouldered between us. I asked how you had been. "Oh...okay," you said, and gave a demonstration smile, as if attesting to the Jim-dandy level of okay-ness you were experiencing. You asked how I had been. This was going well.

"Y'know...working," I said. "I'm working."

I couldn't stop staring at you. Time had lightly notched the skin at the corners of your eyes, but you remained an extraordinarily beautiful woman. You had on a plaid blouse and a wraparound skirt. Traveling clothes. On your right calf, two inches below the knee, was a faded dime-sized bruise. I wanted to touch it.

"I'm doing a piece on smuggling in South Florida," I said.

You told me you had been attending a conference in Miami and had been taking a drive up the coast before returning to California. Then the hurricane alert.

"I'm tenured now. A full professor." You pronounced this last with a lilt, as if to ridicule its freight of pomposity. "I'm only teaching one class this semester, so I've had time to do some writing... a little traveling."

You fitted your eyes to the corner of the bed. Everything was beginning to feel sad and heavy. I kept expecting the climate of bad timing and tragic mistakes that governed our relationship to settle over us and, being unable to generate a reasonable catastrophe on short notice, perform a magical operation that would cause one of us to vanish. You glanced at me. Your smile flickered on, off, on. Off.

"Isn't the hotel awful?" You patted the bed. "These sheets... I don't think they were washed. And I found dead bugs in the bathroom."

"They got tree frogs in the Fontainebleau," I said. "Every hotel in Florida has a signature pest."

You sighed, and I recalled your extensive vocabulary of sighs. This one I interpreted to signify your feeling that I did not sufficiently credit the importance of hotel cleanliness. The conversation required a restart. Would I oblige?

"Want to go for a walk?" I asked.

You didn't quite jump to your feet, but you moved pretty damn fast.

I'VE SAID THAT YOU MAY NOT REMEMBER our time together in Piersall, or more precisely, in the strangely elusive country that Piersall became for several days. Yet perhaps you do remember. Perhaps the memories are troublesome for you. That is why I have been reluctant to write—I doubt the story of those days will have any good effect. It may even cause you harm. Whatever the case, I need your help in determining what has happened to us, and what is happening. If I am to persuade you to help, if you do not remember, then I need to tell you everything, even the most intimate details. It is essential that you accept the fact of our intimacy, because the quality and particulars of that intimacy comprise a large portion of what I want to understand; and the only hope I have of convincing you is to make you aware of what we did and how we were and what we said to one another.

It grew dark as we strolled along the beach. There were no stars, no moon, but a stretch of mucky sand in front of the boardwalk was redly lit by the neon facade of the Joyland Arcade, which was sandwiched between a smallish Ferris wheel and a shop that sold spray-painted hats and T-shirts during the summer. Steps led up to the boardwalk, and we sat on the bottom one and talked. Soon you began to laugh, to lean toward me. Once you touched me on the arm when I made a joke. After that you became less talkative and less affection-ate, and I concluded that you were afraid of encourag-ing me. I felt the same as I had when I first met you. Unnaturally alert and focused. Wavelets slopped onto shore, digital bleeps issued from the arcade, and a warm breeze carried smells of fried food and brine. But I am aware of these things by process of deduction alone—I was completely concentrated on you, atten-tive to every gesture, every nuance of expression.

Years ago you told me that you were painfully shy as a child, afraid of talking, and so had learned to communicate with your eyes—this the reason for their expressiveness. Large and dark, framed by long lashes, they have always had the capacity to calm me, and this potency had been refined when, seven years before, I was jailed in China on a bogus charge of espionage and beaten by the police so badly that I suffered a spinal injury. During my incarceration, to distract my attention from the pain in my back, I would bite my arm until I drew blood. On one occasion I knocked myself out, banging my head so hard against the concrete floor that I was concussed and couldn't see straight for a couple of days. Seeking a less destructive form of pain management, I set about to reconstruct your image from memory. I had intended to recreate your entire body, but once I succeeded in conjuring up your eyes, I abandoned the rest of the project. Thereafter, whenever the guards came into my cell, I would switch on your eyes and watch fragments of light swimming up toward their surfaces, like the bubbles of a diver rising from the depths. Sitting on the boardwalk steps that night, I could scarcely look away from them, and I believed you were using them to warn me off, to tell me that nothing could happen here, nothing had changed, neither your decision to stay with your husband nor the fact that you loved me.

For the better part of an hour you talked about your students—your favorites, others that posed a challenge—and told me news about parents, sisters, pets. Safe topics. But then we touched on the old days. Just dipping our toes in those waters…or so I presumed.

"I ran into Carol a few months ago," you said. "She works in San Francisco now. For a publishing trade paper."

"Carol…huh."

I had lost track of the friends we kept when we were lovers, and I did a lousy impression of someone interested in Carol. The feelings about you that I'd tried to bury had kicked off their shroud and were doing the freak in my head. To hell with Carol. The only person I was interested in was inches away and utterly beyond reach. If we had been characters in a cartoon, a little devil child would have been hopping up and down on my left shoulder, jabbing my head with a pitchfork and screaming, "Grab her!" while on the other shoulder a precious angel baby would have been sprinkling stardust down onto my crotch, reminding me to think pure thoughts and pay no attention to my metabolism, which was throwing a testosterone party. This shit, I told myself, was the very essence of pathetic fucked-uppedness. All I could think to say was something about how I had not seen Carol for years. I couldn't bring myself to sound so banal, so I said something truly stupid instead.

"I still love you, y'know," I said.

You ducked your head. "I know."

Just the response I'd been hoping for.

"Sorry," I said. "I'm ... sorry."

"Russell..." You laid a consoling hand on my shoulder, and I stiffened with resentment—consolation was not required

"It's okay ... I'm fine. Really." With studied nonchalance, I said, "So what did you and Carol get up to?"

"We don't have to talk about Carol," you said.

Somebody inside Joyland switched on the outside speakers, and Bob Marley took to exhorting folks to stand up for their rights.

"I'm probably too worked up to talk about anything else," I said. "I wasn't expecting to see you. I'm not prepared."

You stared off to sea. A played-out wave spread into

a film that raced halfway up the slope of the beach, leaving a line of foam to mark its reach. The pause grew uncomfortably long.

"Why don't we get something to eat?" I said. "I hear Piersall's got great restaurants. Denny's...I heard the Denny's here is truly outstanding."

You gave me a look that I recognized—the sort of distressed look I associated with moments when you had been trying to find a way not to say something hurtful. I'd had occasion in the past, when I was angry, to think that if you spent less time trying not to hurt people, you would do far less damage; but I knew things were more complicated than that.

"I'm not unhappy to see you," you said.

The comment embodied a baffling neutrality—I failed in my attempt to analyze it.

"Me neither," I said. "I'm extremely not unhappy."

That got me a smile.

"Spectacularly not unhappy," I said.

We had maneuvered past the moment, but could not put it completely aside. Our talk grew slower, more considered, and our eyes met frequently, as if we were monitoring levels of intimacy.

"What'll you do once you're finished down here?" you asked.

"Go back to New York. Get another assignment." I flicked a fragment of coquina shell off the step—bits of shell were embedded decoratively in the cement. "There's this guy, this jazz musician...Elliott Crain?"

You weren't familiar with Elliott.

"He's a great guitarist...has his own studio. We've been talking about recording a CD of spoken word stuff. I might take some time and do that. And I've got a book coming out in December. I'm going on kind of a mini-tour."

"That's wonderful!"

You leaned toward me and, I think, were tempted to break the moratorium on touching. You questioned me about the book and the tour, about various writers and film people of my acquaintance whose names came up in the course of conversation.

"You're so busy," you said enviously, as if being busy were an unrealized goal.

"I might take a few weeks after Christmas and go somewhere."

"A vacation?" You laughed. "Where would you go?

You must have been almost everywhere by now."

"Some places are worth a second visit." I wanted to kick myself. Why is it, when you are trying to show a woman that you're an ordinary guy and not an obsessed idiot, every sentence that pops out of your mouth sounds like smooth talk from a bad movie? Maybe, I thought, it was just the obsessed idiot in me.

"They may have changed," you said. "You might not enjoy them as much as you did the first time."

Then again, I thought, maybe you had a similar problem.

I might have extended the metaphor, said something on the order of, "Some places change for the better," and you might have said, "Yes, but such places are often cheapened by tourism," and then we would have gone winging off into an insane approximation of a Monty Python skit. But we were spared this by the appearance of three teenage boys, bagging and sagging in oversized clothes, who leaned on the railing above us and began passing a joint. Their voices were thick and loutish. Their laughter had an impaired quality. Once they finished smoking, they cracked open a couple of forty-ouncers. They peered at us and spoke in an unfamiliar language. It sounded East Asian. Words that dovetailed into sighs and frequently rose in pitch at the end of a phrase. But since the three boys were Caucasian, I decided the language was more likely Eastern European, though that didn't ring true, either.

It became obvious they found our act more entertaining than yet another game of Quake. They were using us for tinder in their search for self-esteem, addressing us in that singsong parlance, then sneering when we failed to respond. Giving up on the idea of a quiet talk, we started back toward Shangri La.

I assumed this would be the extent of our reunion— a chance meeting, a superficial conversation, an exchange of vibrations, all followed by a sleepless night spent separated from you by six inches of plaster and dead bugs. But as we drew near the hotel, its lights illuminating a section of beach, you slipped your hand into mine. You didn't look at me, just kept walking with your head down. Like a fool, I let this state of affairs continue for half a minute or so, supposing that it must be a balance thing—could be you were having difficulty with your footing and had latched on to me for support. The second I smartened up I stepped in front of you and took you by the waist. "Where are we going here?" I asked.

Your right hand fell to my forearm, strayed to my elbow; then you disengaged and walked off toward the water. A breeze fiddled with your hair.

When I was a gun-loving little kid, my uncle used to take me hunting, and I recall standing stock-still and silent so as not to spook the deer grazing on the far side of a creek. I had that feeling now. One twig crack or cough, and you'd bound away into the forest. But I was afraid that stress had frozen your mechanisms, jammed your gears—I had to do something. "Hey," I said, easing up beside you. "Tell me what's going on."

"I'm . . . I don't know what I'm doing," you said.

I shoveled up a toeload of wet sand with my left shoe and flipped it away.

"What are you thinking about?" you asked.

"This second? I was thinking about the last time I saw you. You came to visit me in Oakland over Christmas, remember? We drove down to Carol's place."

"I remember," you said. "You were so desperate."

"I had reason. You wouldn't even kiss me. Just these little pecks on the lips."

"You had so much power over me. I was afraid to kiss you."

Implying, I thought, that I no longer had such power.

"I wish..." You left the words hanging, but I knew more-or-less what you had intended to say—you wished we had made love that night at Carol's, or that you had run away with me to Bali or Bahia or Oregon, or else it was one of a hundred other wishes that could easily have come true.

"If wishes were horses..." I said to fill in the gap.

"Then I'd own the ranch!" You made a comically sad face, and a little "oh well" noise with your lips.

We were stalled, it seemed. Going nowhere slow.

"Have you ever been back to Bahia?" you asked.

"Since I wrote you about it? No."

"I loved your letters."

"I wish I hadn't had to write them."

"The letters I liked best were stories," you said wistfully. "You made up stories about us...as if we were living together in Brazil. Remember? They were so beautiful."

A film of dark water edged with foam seethed up

the incline of the beach; some tiny thing that had been tumbled out of the depths now went skittering back into the sea. I fumbled for your hand. You gave my fingers a squeeze and moved away.

"Want to go for a swim?" I asked.

You gave a startled laugh and said, "Excuse me?"

"Want me to go away?"

"No!" Then, less emphatically, "No...I don't."

"So if you have a choice between going for a swim tonight or me going away, you're down for the swim, right?"

"Is that my choice?" you said distantly. "I'm afraid I didn't bring a suit."

I gestured at the hotel. "They're all watching 'Jeopardy' in there. Nobody'll see us."

A warm rush of wind came from the southeast, and the palms along the beach gave it a hissing, clattering voice, like a convention of witches rustling their broomsticks in applause.

"I don't think so," you said.

I was out of tricks, out of idle conversation. We were here alone together, about to take a step, or else your husband had joined us on the beach in spirit, in

20

which case I was the only one alone. "Well," I said, "if we're not going swimming..."

"Is that really what you want?" you asked.

The tone of your question was annoyed—I wasn't sure how to respond. "I want *something*," I told you. "What do you want?"

"Nothing I do is going to make you happy." You tossed this out there like a handful of dirt on a coffin lid.

"I wasn't figuring on happiness," I said.

The wind dragged its tail across the sand, filling the air with grit. My defeated mood must have been visible, because something surfaced in your expression that partnered it, that acknowledged the awfulness of the circumstance, and you said with exasperation, the words also embodying a gentler form of acquiescence, "If that's what you want, I'll do it for you."

I had been grasping at straws, hoping that my less-than-serious challenge might prolong the conversation. The notion that you would strip off your clothes on a public beach went contrary to what I knew of your character. Yet that is what you did. You unbuttoned your blouse and unwrapped your skirt and proceeded to remove your bra and panties, displaying a put-upon attitude all the while, and yet your actions, while methodical, were not devoid of a seductive element. I suspect you may have known in the back of your mind that your exasperation was in part a pretense, a defense against guilt, or maybe against a lack of guilt. But at the time I was startled, bewildered, and unable to consider such things.

The first time I saw you naked, I was lying on your bed in a dorm room at the University of Wisconsin, where we had met while attending a conference on international journalism—you'd been thinking about switching from a doctorate program in economics to a discipline that would carry you wider afield and thus farther from your marriage. You came out of the bathroom wearing a robe, and when you let it slip from your shoulders, you shot me an apologetic look, as if you assumed I would be disappointed with you.

This time there was no apologetic look. You seemed confident, easier with the idea of nudity. Your breasts were fuller, your hips more voluptuous, but their effect upon me was identical to what I had experienced eleven years before. I felt stupefied, drugged by whiteness, by long, long legs and a high, narrow waist, by everything about you. I've written the word "beautiful" thousands of times in relation to innumerable subjects, but no matter in what context I use the word, when I think of it I remember you as you looked upon our first night, shy and though technically not a virgin, virginal in every other aspect; and I remember as well what might be an illustration from a nineteenth century novel about colonials stranded on a wild shore— a lovely naked woman with one hand lifted to push aside her windblown hair, standing forth from a background of darkly waving palms and night, gazing with calm observance at a bearded man who, judging by his astonished expression, can see nothing but her light.

Your face hardened under my stare, though not in anger. It seemed more a paving over of emotion, of something you wanted to reign in. You stepped from your shoes and ran into the water, breasting the surf in a flat dive and vanishing. I shucked my clothes, did a hopping trouser-removal dance, and followed, plunging through low rollers and swimming hard until I had cleared the break. The water was warm, chest-deep, and silky black. The visibility near zero. I thought of *Jaws*. A thrill rippled the muscles of my neck. Submerged beasts were gliding around me. This was a dumb idea. "Kay!" I shouted. Then I spotted you bobbing an arms-length away, submerged to your shoulders. Unsmiling. I assumed you were about to say something like, "Okay...can we go in now?" but I beat you to the punch and asked if you were cold.

"No, it's nice," you said diffidently.

A swell pushed us together. Your body was smooth, breasts slippery and nudge-soft. I gathered your waist with my right arm and drew you close. My erection prodded between your thighs, and you relaxed against me, your head resting on my shoulder. Either a surrender or an admission. Another swell floated us off our feet, and I lodged the slightest bit inside you. You whispered something as I went deeper, but the soft crush of the surf covered the words. Your breath sang in my ear. A dozy warmth came to cloud me. I had a confused sense of boundary, of position. Both our hearts seemed to be beating in my chest. The swells heaved, carrying us up from the bottom, and we would drift along in a dreamlike union until our feet found new ground. The first time this happened, you clutched at me in alarm, pulling my head under, and I swallowed a mouthful of salty water. But soon you adapted, adjusting your movements to the greater movement that enclosed us. I could barely see your face, but I felt your self, your soul, shifting toward me, the barrier of absence and dead time that had grown between us beginning to crumble. It was as if I were making love to the ocean, as if the Gulf had evolved a female form and fitted her to me and infused her with your spirit. Before long, I surrendered to her my own measure of salt.

Afterward we dressed quickly, silently. I wanted to talk to you, but you projected a unapproachable exterior and refused to look at me. We barefooted it across the lawn toward the hotel. The senior citizen behind the desk, an ungainly liver-spotted stick of man wearing a Marlins cap and suspenders over his undershirt, tracked us with robotic steadiness as we hustled through the lobby in our wet clothes. The elevator was as old as the night man, a scarred yellow on the inside. You watched the arrow above the doors—it barely moved, registering a slow, shuddering progress. I felt more cut off from you than I had earlier. Just before the doors opened, you said, "Is this enough for you? If it's just tonight...can you accept that?"

"Probably not," I said. "But what am I going to do?"

IF I HAD STEPPED BACK FROM THE MOMENT, I might have noticed how conflicted you were and realized that I should go slowly. But I believed you had reached the same level of assurance I had, and once we had showered I laid you down on your bed and kissed your mouth, your neck, your breasts. Every inch with its own flavor. The back of one knee still bearing a trace of saltiness; the point of your right hip flowery from the bathwater; the soft skin of your inner thighs like warm vanilla. When I fluttered my tongue along the folds of your cunt, your hips bridged up, your stomach muscles tightened. You released a shivery sigh. I licked the interior of your lips the way a cat laps around the rim of a bowl, then took them in my mouth. Velvety and damp. Like holding a crushed rose on my tongue. I licked you again, opening you completely, and slipped a finger inside. Your musk was in my throat, my nostrils. You tensed when I came near your clitoris, and I thought this was a signal that you wanted me there. I worked a second finger inside you and thrust in and out with a deliberate rhythm, now and again replacing my fingers with the stiffened tip of my tongue, nourishing your anticipation. You were trembling. Little seismic quivers and tensings. I could hear your voice—not what you were saying, only its urgency. And then, to my utter bewilderment, you were pushing my head away with the heel of your hand.

"Kay?" I got to my knees. There was just enough light from the street for me to see you. Your eyes glistened with tears. "What's the matter?" I asked, settling beside you. I rested a hand on your shoulder.

You were speechless in misery.

"Tell me what's wrong," I said.

You closed your eyes. "It's all right," you said in a small, shaky voice. But it obviously wasn't all right.

I began to have the kind of thoughts I'd had in the days after you had told me you were returning to your marriage, but before you actually left me. Angry thoughts. Thoughts about your husband and how he manipulated you. Thoughts arising from helplessness, from being filled with a powerful energy that demanded release, and having no fruitful use for it, no purpose to sustain it. I asked if you wanted me to leave. You shook your head, clamped my hand against your shoulder. I put an arm around you, and you turned your back so I could hold you as I might a child, close and confining, becoming a shelter in which— after not so long a time—you fell asleep, retreating from guilt or whatever phantom it was that had brought you to tears.

I was tired, but my mind was active, questing about for an answer that would satisfy the confusion of the night, wondering what had happened, what it signified and where it would lead, going an aimless circuit of anxiety and frustration. I wanted to penetrate the borders of your sleeping mind and find the secret you were keeping, and maybe also discover the secret that had kept us apart for so many years. I knew you well, knew you in ways no one else did, and given what you had told me of your marriage, its passionless character, I could not understand what held you there. The reasons you had offered ("I care about him;" "I'll hurt so many people;" and so on) were good and proper reasons, yet they seemed insufficient in face of the unhappiness you expressed and a life you had described as a "colorless nightmare." And so I had concluded that you must distrust me on some important level—I wanted to find the reason for that, too. Hours like this. Round and round, unable to stop. Content to be holding you, yet plagued by discontent. I didn't fall asleep until the sky began to gray and I heard gulls in the offing, shrieking over fish, and my thoughts dissolved in a solution of sadness and fatigue.

WHEN I WOKE THE NEXT MORNING you weren't in the room. I thought you must have stolen off and were halfway to Miami in your rental car. Then I spotted your suitcase and was relieved, though I realized I needed to prepare myself for your departure. Ten minutes later you returned. "The phones are dead," you said, setting your purse down on the dresser. "Even cell phones. There's an atmospheric disturbance of some kind." You sat in the chair by the window. "The roads are out, too." You seemed upset, but less so than you might have been.

"The hurricane?" I asked, and you nodded glumly.

"But we didn't get any rain." I sat up. "Or wind. Did you hear any wind?"

"The desk clerk says all the damage happened north and south of Piersall."

"Weird. I didn't think hurricanes worked like that." I flicked the switch of the lamp on the bedside table and the bulb glowed.

"The town has its own generator," you said.

"According to the desk clerk?"

Another glum nod. "He said we could be here another two or three days."

A motor scooter passed outside, like the ripping down of a zipper amplified a million times. Silence filled in after it.

"Are you all right?" I asked.

You looked puzzled.

"Last night," I said. "When I was making love with you…"

I thought I detected the beginnings of a morose expression, but you ordered your face and said, "I'm okay."

"Did I do something?"

"Oh, no! It was…"

You appeared to be searching for the right words.

"Never mind," I said. "If you're okay…"

"...a control issue," you said.

I could make no sense of the response. I was certain it related to your ball and chain, the pale gray ghost of the man you married extending an ectoplasmic finger of reproval. But I understood how guilt worked in you—I knew your guilt would be intricate.

Another silence was heading our way. "Why don't we get some food," I said. "We can talk over breakfast."

You remained downcast for a moment, then allowed yourself a twenty-five watt smile. "Denny's," you said crisply.

"Don't worry. I've got pills that'll protect us." I swung my legs out from beneath the covers. "Let me grab a shower."

NOT MANY FOLKS WERE OUT AND ABOUT in Piersall that morning, and the Denny's, which probably depended on people passing through town for most of its business, was serving only three other customers: a thirtyish couple and their toddler daughter. Two waitresses were sitting at a rear table, smoking and reading tabloids. Once our food arrived I found myself watching your hands as you buttered your toast. They made every act seem graceful. Elegant, long-fingered ladies in themselves. Perfect, I thought, for weaving sorrow into time. I remembered how they touched me.

The waitress, a beefy girl in a brown and beige uniform, mosied over to our booth, popped her gum and asked, "How y'all doin'?"

We both said, "Fine."

"My sandwich looks like the picture on the menu," I said as the waitress wandered away. "Maybe they airbrush the food."

You gave a polite laugh, a spoonful of sound.

On the street outside, a battered white pickup truck rattled past, carrying a gabble of grubby kids in back, trailing a plume of dark smoke. The toddler started crying, and the cook came out of the kitchen and leaned on the cash register, gazing mournfully out at the fog, the listless palms and the leaden waters of the Gulf.

After a considerable break in our conversation, you said distractedly, "There's nothing I can do." I wasn't certain you knew that you had spoken out loud. You bit your lower lip—a self-conscious gesture that made you seem very young—and looked to me for a reaction.

"No," I said, not wanting to appear elated. "I don't think so."

You cut a bite of omelet. "As soon as they fix the roads I've got to ..."

"I know. I'll deal with it," I said.

You chewed the bite and swallowed, then said briskly, "What should we do first?'

Then you blushed.

"Dumb question," you said.

We finished eating, and the beefy waitress approached, bearing the check. "So what's there to do in Piersall?" I asked her.

She eyed me with displeasure. "You're a funny fella," she said, and ambled off to rejoin her sisters in food service limbo.

"We should change hotels," you said with some firmness. Your advocacy of this cause doubtless inspired by the dead bugs.

"There may not be another hotel."

"I passed a TraveLodge on the way in."

"TraveLodges aren't off-limits to palmetto bugs."

"At least the sheets will be fresh."

"Not for long," I said.

33

TEN IN THE MORNING, with the gray drapes closed, we stood in the center of our room at the TraveLodge, embracing in an artificial greenish twilight. I unbuttoned your blouse, unhooked your brassiere. You smiled a coy seductress smile and held out your arms so I could pull the straps free. Your breasts cozied in my palms. Soon all our clothing was puddled on the floor. You were quickly ready, angling up onto your toes to let me inside. I cupped your buttocks, drew you closer. The feeling of your body against mine was heady, all fine and familiar. I was lost in your warmth, your scent, and I imagined that we were merging. Two hot ghosts standing together, melting into the same space.

How many times, I wonder, have we made love? It's difficult to reckon with any accuracy, because many of our encounters have encompassed a considerable passage of time and multiple couplings. But even if the definition by which I arrive at the sum is a liberal one, it would not be so many. Surely far less than the number of times we have made love to other partners. Yet those occasions stand out like constellations in a sky of lesser involvements, and of *that* number there are several deserving of a sky all their own. That morning in the Piersall TraveLodge took its place in the pantheon, enshrined in a section given over to Swiss Chalets and Red Roof Inns and Best Westerns, all incidents noteworthy for having transcended their surroundings. There were still barriers between us, but they weren't important to the moment, and together we became the person we always managed to become when we lay down and looked so closely at each other that differences and barriers and the concept of distance itself seemed elements of the geography of a country we had left far behind. The things you said to me in your passion were things I would have said—you said them for us—and when I pulled you atop me or turned you onto your side, I was enacting the mechanical principles of our singular desire. Nothing is perfect. No object, action, or idea. Yet in the brilliant ease and intensity of our union we felt perfected, we felt each other give way completely in the service of a heated oblivion where we lived a certain while. I remember there was music, and yet there was no music, only whispers and breath and the background drone of some humming TraveLodge machine whose cycles came to have the complexity and depth of a raga. I remember a soft white light around us that likely did not exist, or else I do not know how it was generated, other than to speculate that our skins were aglow or weeping melanin. What did exist, what was made of us, and what we were for that time, I cannot call to mind. Love's creature lives beyond memory and in the absolute. I only recall its colors.

Sometime late that afternoon we slept, and when I waked I found the green twilight had not changed its shade. I stretched, yawned, and noticed you lying on your side, watching me. I turned over and kissed you.

"You want to sleep more?" I asked.

"No," you said. "I'm…"

"What?"

You shook your head, as if to suggest that what you were doing or feeling was inexpressible. Happiness was in your face, but I knew it was only a weather passing through. I propped myself on an elbow, ran a hand along your hip, spread my fingers on your thigh.

"What are you thinking?" you asked.

"I'm reciting my mantra," I said.

You made as if to pinch my hand. "Tell me!"

"I was thinking how your face looks when I'm inside you."

"How does it look?"

"Like you're straining to hear something. A voice. Music. Like you can't quite hear it clearly."

You shut your eyes. "I'm not seeing it."

"You look kinda goofy."

You laughed. "That sounds closer to the truth."

I slid my hand between your thighs—the skin there was moist. You clamped your legs together, imprisoning my fingers.

"You still sensitive?" I asked.

"Nope." You relaxed your legs, clamped them together again. "It feels like it's glowing."

"Actually," I said, "it is. I can see a beam of light. Somebody's trapped down there."

You gave me a playful smack.

"They could be in danger," I said. "I should investigate."

"You've done enough investigating. By now I should think you'd be familiar with my every nook and cranny."

"That's no way for a professor to talk," I said.

We nodded off once more, lying spoon style, and when I waked after an hour or thereabouts, we had not changed position. I grew hard again and although half-asleep, you allowed me to penetrate you—such a sterile term for so pure an acceptance. I was sleepy myself, and I had a corresponding sense of primitive intimacy, as if my hips were guided more by force of natural law than by conscious desire. I imagined we were two inert bodies that had drifted together and were rocking on the same tide. An almost restful sort of lovemaking. At last I rolled away from you and onto my back. Flashes of light pricked the darkness behind my eyelids. A residue of thought circled the drain.

You twisted about onto your stomach and rested your chin on my bicep. "You didn't finish."

"Nuh-uh."

"I wanted you to."

"It's all right," I said. "You know. Spirit's willing but…"

"The flesh is weak?"

"Not weak," I said. "It's on hiatus."

You kissed me on the forehead, the mouth, and

then I felt you stroking me, restoring my erection. "It doesn't feel on hiatus to me," you said.

"What're you up to?"

"Playing." Your fingers tightened. "Do you mind?"

"Mmmn-mm."

"Is that a yes?"

"Yeah, I can take it."

"You just think you can," you said.

You got to your hands and knees, positioning yourself so that your breasts swayed against my cock, letting it rub against them, slide between them...like being caressed by doves. And then your lips enclosed me. You had been less adventurous when I knew you years before, and I wondered fleetingly if another man had changed your attitudes, and I envied all the imaginary lovers with whom I now populated your sexual history. Soon I reached out to you and warned you I was going to come, uncertain whether this was what you wanted. You trapped my hand and interlaced your fingers with mine. Your lips tightened, gliding the length of me and back; your tongue swirled, and the sensation of urgency in my groin congealed into something more demanding. Perhaps because of my envies and concerns, my outcry seemed unnaturally hoarse and ugly, like that of a desolate starving creature celebrating a great prize that he had unearthed from a barren field.

I pulled you close and we lay entwined in greenish twilight. When I kissed you I tasted myself warm on your lips. Minutes slowed. The white bed drifted. We lay becalmed, and I began to dissolve in you again. Everywhere I aimed my eyes I found no end to happiness or time. Hope and despair in equal balance. Small worries flittered above a central thought, like birds circling above an island: What was this matter in us that survived without air or light, and lived so fiercely on and on, determined to recreate itself? Then thought flew south. In the street a child's voice shrilled. Out in the corridor an elevator bonged. We slept at the cool, luminous center of the world. All fear surrendered. All our life of trouble, gone.

DURING THE NEXT TWO DAYS AND NIGHTS we rarely left that anonymous little room with its bolted windows and dead cold air. We redecorated it with discarded clothing and take-out containers, but it never acquired the least vitality or charm. The best that can be said was that at times it had the decency to cease to exist and let us not feel imprisoned. We needed privacy, and not merely for making love, but to become reacquainted, to talk. Some of the talk dealt with old memories, some with what we each had been doing. But much of it was frivolous, playful. Medicine for us. I could feel the scars where we had been torn apart softening, the fresh tissues merging, annealing, and establishing new and improved connections.

"Remember the pictures you sent me when my back was fucked up?" I asked at one point. I was lying on my stomach, an arm across your breasts. "You sent me this one...you were wearing a red top. Just the top. You were in your kitchen, smiling and showing off your legs."

"Uh-huh," you said blithely. "You liked it."

"I had a hard-on for a week."

"I guess that was my intention," you said. "Although I wasn't thinking in such clinical terms."

"Maybe you were and just didn't know it." I pushed myself around to lean my head against your shoulder.

"Were you wearing panties under the top?"

You gave me an arch look. "I'll never tell."

"I didn't figure you would."

"Why's that?"

"The way you were smiling...in the picture. I'd say it was designed to make me consider the question."

"Maaay-be!" You turned it into a two-note song.

"I say no," I said.

"No what?"

"No panties. You look embarrassed...just a little. Like this is your first time doing soft porn. I don't think you're a good enough actress to be faking it."

You affected dismay. "You don't respect my talent?"

"Baby," I said, doing my Tom Waits impression, "anybody can have talent. That's not the important thing."

"And what's the important thing?"

"That you're not wearing panties now."

"I don't have any!" You gave me a look of such solemnity, you might have been asking me to take a vow. "We *have* to do a laundry."

I was startled. "Right now?"

You stretched like a lazy kitten curled in a ball, and in the same movement, brought your fingers to my cheek as if reaching out touch a catnip mouse, loving it, but too tired to play.

"Un-uh," you said. "Just sometime."

WHILE YOU WERE DROWSING, I experienced one of those unexpected cracks in the world that lets you perceive essentials. It seemed I was looking along the corridor of your life, past career-marriage-love, past the legend of your cloistered youth and fairy-tale-princess childhood, past moments like stained glass windows and others like boarded-up doors, past party dresses, mini-skirts, academic gowns, past tics and tempers, minor disorders, all the pointless behaviors that seek to define us. Seeing you this way, the way you would look to God if He was a maker of small delicate machines and was into examining his work, hunched over a bench with a jeweler's glass, I realized that your systematic progression from child to schoolgirl to college student to wife and womanhood was marred by a single mutant disruption: Me. And this led me to analyze the desultory and intemperate character of my own life, to view myself as unsuitable and of lesser substance. As a consequence, when you stirred and stretched, I started talking about some bullshit thing that I hoped would impress you with its quirky charm, convince you that the vivid, untutored spirit with whom you had fallen in love still existed, as if to my mind it did not and never had.

"Want to hear my theory of the personality?" I asked.

The pillow muffled your answer.

"You know what color wheels are? Those cardboard wheels with colored plastic panels...they use them in clubs, spin 'em around in front of spotlights? Personalities are like color wheels. A little more complicated. Same principle, though."

"You should publish," you said dryly. "It's brilliant."

"See, we're each born with certain colors. Maybe that's what people who see auras see. Whatever, most people—if they bought into the analogy—would believe that these colors can be dirtied. Spoiled. But that's not so. They can be destroyed, the panel can be broken. But if they aren't broken, they stay with us. So"—I gave your hip a quick rub, as if buffing a magic lamp—"I'm here to tell you, all your colors are intact."

You blinked, focused on me.

"It's pre-Freudian," I said. "Kind of a Gnostic interpretation."

You brushed my chin with your fingertips, as if to assure yourself that I was really there. You looked vaguely worried.

"What's wrong?" I asked.

"Nothing."

I tried to make out what the problem was by studying your face. "I know what this is," I said. "The old thing about we're too different to live together. Intellectually incompatible. How you go like, A plus B times the coefficient of an unknown beta, and I do shit like throw magic beans up in the air to learn the secrets of my enemies."

As I spoke you were shaking your head.

"What then . . . what is it?"

"It's nothing," you said in a faded voice; you were still staring at me.

I tried to reset the conversation, but I had lost my train of thought. "What was I saying?"

"About the magic beans?" You sounded distant in a Valium sort of way.

"No...before."

"I don't know. Oh! The color wheel thing, you mean?"

"Yeah, that's it," I said.

I had lost interest in persuading you of anything. It troubled me that I had so little self-confidence. Though I had long since determined the root cause— an abusive parent—I often forgot its capacity to undermine and devalue. The color wheel thing, for instance. I had been bullshitting, of course, but it was nonetheless representative of how I viewed the world, of an intellectual apparatus I had jury-rigged out of things half understood to compensate for a lack of formal education, the magpie creation of a savage confronted by the need to pass for civilized. Yet I had offered it as parody, as whimsy, because I tended to suspect that everything I said or did was somehow a fraud. Every achievement the result of a trick I had played on reality. You, on the other hand, thought everything you said and did was at least an attempt to be truthful. Not that you hadn't told some lies. But you believed so strongly in your innate honesty, when it came to the gray areas, those situations in which no one can know whether what they're doing is or is not an operation of the truth, on those occasions you chose to believe your judgments were commensurate with the truth. It was a good way to be, and I envied you for it, even though that quality in you had caused me a great deal of pain.

I asked again what you had been worrying about. You laid your palm against my cheek and said, "It's nothing bad about you...I promise." Your eyes cooled me and in a grave, quiet voice not even I could entirely disbelieve, you said, "I think you're wonderful."

OUR SECOND AFTERNOON AT THE TRAVELODGE, we sat side by side on the bed, working on our laptops. It was, I believe, a pretense of normalcy. We were playing house, pretending to live the life into which our relationship should have evolved. You were making notes for a paper on nuclear politics. I typed away at my article, but grew bored and began to make my own notes, which included the following:

Every time I lie down with you, it makes me think
of kids who've pulled a blanket over their heads,
creating a warm and secret place, with too much
wriggling going on, too many arms and legs to fit
into such a small enclosure. Until we fit together,
that is. From that point on, the space enclosing us
seems to become both infinitely large and infinitely
small, a compacted vastness in which we entwine
like lovers in a cosmic egg.

"THAT'S NOT YOUR ARTICLE," you said, peering at my screen.

You tried to tug the laptop from me, but I held onto it. "Let me see!" you said, and when I refused, you relinquished your grip and said, "If you're going to write about us, I should be allowed to read it."

I gestured at your laptop and said, "I'll trade you."

You thought it over. "All right."

On the screen was a short poem entitled "On Erections:"

When I was ten, they were mythical beasts, capable
of unimaginable feats.

*When I was sixteen, they were charming, though a
    little bit alarming.*

*When I was twenty, they were threatening, by thirty
    often deadening.*

*But then I found you, and when I did I knew they
    were neither better nor worse than who they were
    attached to.*

I was surprised—I was accustomed to being the poem-writer in the relationship. It felt strange to be the one celebrated. It felt good.

"Do you like it?" you asked.

"Yeah," I said, reading it again. "Nobody ever wrote me a poem before."

"If I were a better writer I'd write you a real poem."

The longer I looked at the words, the more I was moved by their specificity, especially by the third line which summarized certain of your attitudes toward the marriage that had caused you so much unhappiness, and that you could not leave. Each line inspired by the man for whom you would not leave it.

"This is a real poem," I said.

You looked pleased.

I read it a third time. The logic of the poem was unassailable. It was less art than a succinct document, and I was tempted to use it as evidence, to let its sad authenticity prove to you that every word it said resonated with a larger truth.

"You wrote this today?" I asked.

You were reading the screen of my laptop. "Uh-huh. I was going to email it to you."

"You don't have my email."

"Yes, I do. I even know where you live."

"I don't think so," I said. "I just moved."

"565 West Eleventh Street. Apartment Two."

"How'd you find out?"

"The internet. I know your cell number, too." You folded your hands on your stomach and regarded me with what I interpreted to be self-satisfaction. "I was thinking about getting in touch."

I absorbed this and said, "What did you have in mind?"

A beat, and then we both laughed. We laughed a long time, and the laughter dispelled—temporarily, at least—whatever tensions were left in us.

"See how it works," I said. "You contemplate something, the world produces it. You rule."

"In this instance," you said, "I guess I do."

We went back to reading each others laptops, and after an interval you asked with mock sternness, "What does this refer to? 'Thick, like the heavy syrup you find at the bottom of a can of peaches.'"

I grinned.

"I'm 'a can of peaches,' am I?"

"Sometimes."

"I think you should rework the metaphor." A half-smile. "You may need to revisit the experience."

"That's what this was about?" I kissed your neck, the top of your shoulder. "You didn't have to go through all that. All you have to do is point."

You pointed.

"Here I go," I said. "Revisiting."

This time your scent was hotter, your taste more tart, and I felt slightly maddened, like a dog feasting on his favorite treat. I licked you roughly, and that's what you needed. No teasing, no anticipation. You wanted it to happen now. Your thighs clamped down, your belly quaked. You sang your little heartbreak pleasure song.

"Like kiwi oil," I said afterward. "Like liquid silk."

"Much better," you said.

We lay quietly for a while, kissing some, and then I said, "Seriously. Why were you thinking about getting in touch?"

"I missed you."

"That's it?"

"I missed you a lot." You kissed my nose. "I think you want to know if there was an inciting incident. In my marriage."

"Yeah, maybe."

"No," you said. "At home it pretty much just goes along."

A homily, I thought, for the twenty-first century. One that would come to replace "Home Is Where The Heart Is." I wanted to say, I don't get it. After six years you just started to miss me? Or did it build up over time? What? But that would have killed the mood.

"I like your poem," I said.

You crossed your arms over your breasts, gave yourself a hug. It looked as if you felt nice and sleepy. Sweet and heavy with juice. Like a can of peaches.

AT DENNY'S THAT NIGHT—I gambled on the turkey tetrazini; you played it conservative with a chef salad—our waitress told us that Piersall had a movie house. The Beach Theater. She didn't know what was playing, but said it was probably something that had shown in Miami the past summer. Then she served my dinner, which proved to be chalky slabs of something dead smothered in an orange-hued sauce. You smirked at me from behind the bastion of your salad. I tried the turkey. The orange sauce was sticky and bland, like melted plastic. I made sure to save room for popcorn.

The Beach was a parcel-shaped building of white stucco with an ornate marquee, its walls postage-stamped with placards variously advertising a gospel concert, a circus, and a candidate for the local school board. The lobby had a faded faux-Victorian ambience that made me imagine men wearing hats and ladies in ankle-length print dresses, smoking cigarettes and watching Bogart and Edward G. Robinson in *Key Largo*. That night's feature was a picture neither of us had heard of—a film entitled *Class*, which turned out to be a remake of J. M. Barrie's *The Admirable Crichton* starring Bruce Willis. "'Gilligan's Island' with a brain" read a blurb on the poster. Apparently neither Gilligan nor British farce had much of a following in Piersall— there were only five other movie lovers in the auditorium. We sat toward the rear, holding hands, watching the previews, the most notable of which was a science fiction film entitled *Denizen,* featuring Dolph Lundgren playing an alien and Tia Carrera as the plucky biologist who loves him—an exemplary non-xenophobic act on her part, as Dolph had a nasty habit of shape-shifting into ever more hideous forms.

Through all our relationship I had previously seen only one movie with you—*My Brilliant Career,* with Sam Neill and Judy Davis. A very good movie, but I paid it scant attention, being overwhelmingly concerned with whether you were going to leave me. Strangely enough, though I believed I would soon lose you again, I enjoyed this experience. Maybe I had learned that it was important to take whatever pleasure of life you could when you found it. Maybe I had become a fatalist. You held my hand in your lap, then lifted it to your lips and kissed my knuckles and gave me a sly smile.

Class got off to a decent start. Willis played Max

Brickowski, a world-class handyman on the estate of thirty-something Silicon Valley billionaire, Nick Bruno (Greg Kinnear). Celebrities were always in evidence about the place, flaunting their gasbag egos. Rock stars, actors, sports figures, et al. Many of them ridiculed Max as he plodded through his day, repairing tennis machines and tractor mowers and so forth. But Nick, though he did not actually respect Max, liked to use him for a sounding board—in his view Max was a dolt with solid instincts, who was honest enough to tell him when he was off-base with an idea. There was some amusing interplay between the various egomaniacs visiting the estate, and then the whole sick crew, ten strong, was away on a Brazilian vacation aboard the private jet, with Max making an eleventh. Nick frequently took him along on trips as a good luck charm. Then a storm, a plane crash on a remote jungle island, and when the rich folks proved themselves inept at survival, Max stepped in to take charge.

(I put an arm about you, my hand dangling, brushing your breast, copping a high-school feel, and you rested your head on my shoulder.)

Once Max had established primacy by rigging

primitive plumbing, finding edible roots, devising animal and fish traps, and spouting homely wisdoms that the rich folks came to regard with the awe of disciples receiving the Word; and after a sub-plot involving potentially hostile, mostly comic-relief natives had been established, romance bloomed between Max and Nick's blueblood girlfriend, Jillian (Gwyneth Paltrow). All the women wanted Max—the tennis star (Anna Kournikova in her film debut); the swimsuit model (Denise Richards); the corporate lawyer (Juliette Lewis); the rock star (Angelina Jolie). But it was Jillian who won Max's heart. Nick—and all the men for that matter—were amusingly depressed and grumbly, but things settled down and finally Max and Jillian shared their first kiss. The kiss was a humdinger, but Jillian, who was a good girl, withheld her favors from the horny handyman.

(In the darkness of the theater, we did our best Max and Jillian impression. Our kiss lasted considerably longer than theirs.)

Trouble came to the island paradise in the form of bungling native attacks and the ominous approach of Nick's business rival (Oliver Platt), who—it developed—had sabotaged the billionaire's jet, thus caus-ing the accident. After having been trounced several times, the natives concluded that Max was the ruler foretold by prophecy. Good-natured and humorous interactions came to be the order of the day between survivors and tribe, the most clever being Nick acting out an episode of Star Trek for the tribal children, a performance that earned him a loyal following.

(I worked a hand along the inside of your thigh, my fingers toying with the elastic band of your panties. I was having something of a confinement problem, and with your left hand, you made an adjustment that helped immensely.)

The villain landed his gilt helicopter on the island, followed in due course by a seaplane that dis-gorged a mercenary force of headset-wearing, pony-tailed assassins armed with automatic rifles and explosive devices. Max, who had earned a Silver Star in Desert Storm, conceived a plan. Survivors and natives alike began boobytrapping the island. Nick's assistant (Robert Downey Jr.) was captured and underwent interrogation—the bad guys gave Robert drugs to destroy his will to resist and he got behind them too heavily to answer questions. Jillian was worried. Max consoled her. With both of them thinking the end was at hand, they went at it like weasels in mating season.

(The limits of heavy petting were getting a workout. You slid forward, allowing my fingers full play. Your mouth was pressed into my shoulder so as to muffle any outcry, and though I would not have thought it likely, it appeared that if things kept going the way they were, the normally demure Dr. Kay Rossman would soon be elevated to member in good standing of the Third-Row-from-the-Back Club.)

Mercenaries fell into pits, were trapped in nets, mugged by spider monkeys, half-drowned in suddenly undammed river courses. All the survivors fought well, and Nick regained the respect of his pals and the love of Ms. Jolie by leading an attack that captured his evil competitor. Almost everyone was happy. The bad guy's radio was used to summon help. Nick promised to provide medical care and a satellite dish for the tribe. The other survivors had grown as people. But Max knew what was coming. Once they returned to civilization he would be right back on the bottom of the heap. He wandered off alone for a last look around his kingdom. Jillian was nowhere to be found.

(You bit my shoulder, made a fuming noise. You pressed your thighs together—to stop me, I imagined. But it was too late. Your hips spasmed, you pushed yourself down onto my fingers and half-turned into me, burying your face in my chest, going crazy in secret.)

Back at the estate a month later, everything was as it had been in the beginning. Max was doing his job...though he had been given notice. Due to their recent history, Nick found Max's presence difficult to bear. He offered to set Max up in business, but Max was thinking about moving on. Jillian was at least formally back with Nick—she wasn't altogether comfortable with this, but she had committed to try and work things out. The other survivors were uneasy around Max. They shunned him.

(You were giving me a rueful look, and I was beginning to recognize certain unhappy resonances between Max's life and my own.)

Max was packing on his last night at the estate, when Jillian appeared in his doorway. Their conversation was strained at first. Remonstrative. But there came a breakthrough, Jillian admitting to herself that she loved Max, and that love was the answer to every human question. They shared a breathtaking kiss. Then in walked Nick and a sampling of the other survivors—when he saw Max and Jillian kissing, he threatened to have Max thrown in jail, and the scene became a spectacle of chest-beating and accusations, until brave little Jillian stepped up to the plate and delivered a soliloquy designed to win the hearts of the Academy, telling Nick and his glitzy buds they should be ashamed! They owed everything to Max (she stamped her pretty foot)! Everything! This segued into a maudlin overview of the inequities of the class system, doubtless written by some ex-left-wing alcoholic hack who wept while typing it. Nick was, indeed, shamed. As were they every one. They embraced Max as one of their own, promised to make his fortune. Now he could be rich like them! But rich or not, you knew Max was way too real to let money change him. As for Jillian, she was awfully sorry, but Nick understood, didn't he? She had to go with her heart, with Max. Nick struggled with this, but he too had grown, and he understood. The delightful Ms. Jolie was hanging all over him, softening the blow. Group hugs, and a big sloppy Jillian kiss for Max. Theme music up. Fade to credits.

Only in Hollywood.

As we exited the theater, in a touching memorial to small town courtesy, the skinny, balding, middle-aged manager stood by the door saying the same thing to each of his five patrons: "Good night. Hope y'all enjoyed the show."

"I should have told him how satisfying it was," you said as we crossed the street, narrow and un-trafficked, lined by darkened glass storefronts that reflected only one another.

"The noise you made, he probably knew."

"I was very discrete."

We walked hand-in-hand without speaking for most of a block, and then you asked, "Do you think Jillian should have gone with Max?"

I hesitated. "That's not such a good question to be asking me."

You looked blank; then you got it. "I wasn't talking about us," you said peevishly. "I was talking about two characters in a movie."

"Uh-huh. You didn't notice any resemblance?"

"I've never thought of you as being someone who repairs small appliances."

"I mean situationally speaking. The triangle. The characters...the types."

"I suppose there's a marginal resemblance."

"If *Class* didn't do it for you," I said, "let's find a video store and rent *Casablanca*. That's my favorite. You fly away to save the planet with Mr. Nobel Peace Prize. I wind up walking off into the fog with the gay French cop."

You repressed a smile; you weren't ready to forgive me. After a break you asked, "Was Claude Rains gay?"

"Christ, I don't know."

"I don't want to fight," you said stiffly.

"Fine by me."

We made it to the end of the block before you spoke again. Then you said, "It's not that I want to go back."

"Sure it is. But every once in a while you *wish* you didn't want to."

"More than that," you said in an injured tone.

"Okay. Twice in a while."

You stopped on the curb. "I think about leaving every day," you said. "I make plans to leave. But whenever I start to take the final step, I just can't hurt him."

I knew that song—"I Just Can't Hurt Him." It had been in heavy rotation the first five years of our relationship. The melody was okay, but the lyrics sucked. The thinking-about-leaving-every-day part, however, that was new.

"What do you want me to say?" I asked. "You want me to argue? I'm out of arguments. I used 'em all up six years ago."

"I don't want you to argue. I want you to understand!"

A young black couple was approaching, and you broke it off. They were walking with their arms around each other, and the girl's head was on the boy's shoulder—she was wearing a University of Miami varsity jacket about ten sizes too large. The boy offered us a soft, "Hello," as they passed, and the girl's eyes swept across us and she smiled sweetly. The peacefulness of their union collapsed the bubble of resentment that had formed around us, and caused me to yearn for innocence and ease.

63

"You seem to think it's just you," you said tearfully. "That it was only hard for you. Leaving you...it was like being ripped apart."

I started to say that it was you who had done the ripping, but I couldn't pull the trigger.

"I didn't know if I could live. Every time Morris touched me, I wanted to throw up. It's better now but...I just can't bear to be in the world without you anymore. I don't know what to do."

So many urgencies contended for my notice, they canceled each other out. I felt emptied, erased. Drops of rain began to speckle the sidewalk, producing numb circles on my skin.

You linked your arms behind my neck, rested your forehead against mine. Everything about you was clear and unmistakable. "I love you," you whispered.

Something burned in my chest, and it was all like hot smoke in my head, a fresh hurt brewing, and I could hardly speak.

"I know," I said.

IN THE MORNING WE BOUGHT fruit and pastries and coffee at a grocery and ate on a bench out front of the Joyland Arcade. A middling surf tumbled in from the fog bank. Reddish brown piles of seaweed littered the beach, humped like bodies of the drowned beneath tattered shrouds. Seagulls keened and skied, pelicans bobbed on the swells, sandpipers left sharp three-toed tracks along the tidal margin. But any notion of nature in harmony took a hit when you factored in the derelict sleeping it off close to the seawall. At casual glance he resembled another pile of seaweed, but then I saw he was wearing a long brown coat, maybe a raincoat, and had many brightly colored bits of paper—like Post-it notes, I thought—stuck to his sleeve.

You were nibbling a slice of pineapple. The breeze handled your hair, lifted the collar of your blouse, and your left hand was posed in a mudra against the lap of your tan slacks. I had a sense I had caught you in a private mood, one I had not seen before, that perhaps no one had seen. There was a calmness collected in your eyes, in the sculpture of your mouth, that seemed altogether unfamiliar, of such magnitude and concentration I didn't believe it would manifest if you were distracted by the presence of a companion. It was as though you had floated away from me, and I was spying on you from cover...I remembered watching a jaguar come down to drink at the margin of a jungle lake in Guatemala, watching a drunk young girl dancing by herself to a jukebox romance in a Guayaquil bar, and other glimpses of the kind, those sudden, secret observances that stay in our minds and somehow connect and sustain the rest of life, as if life were a fabric and they were the pins it was stretched between. It was like that watching you as I sipped my coffee, on the bench beside you, hidden from your sight.

You set the pineapple slice on a napkin, reached into the pastry sack. "Aren't you hungry?" you asked.

"Welcome back," I said.

"I wasn't anywhere. Actually,"—you chose a croissant—"I was thinking about New York."

"What about it?"

"Just remembering...different things."

"Which ones."

"Going to the jazz club with your friends. The first time we made love in your apartment..." You broke an end off the croissant and nibbled.

"Know what I think about first thing when I think

66

about New York? The day you arrived, kissing you under the big oak tree down by the softball field."

"Oh, yeah." You went there for a moment, had another bite of croissant. "This is like the old joke... about the comedians who know each other's jokes so well, they refer to them by number to get a laugh."

"Thirty-four," I said, and you pretended to swoon.

You looked at me fondly. "I like being with you now better than I did in New York. We're finally getting to know each other. Before there was always so much pressure."

"Yeah, it was a lot worse back then—the pressure."

"I think it helps we're older." You dusted crumbs from your hands. "I'm more independent, and you"— you tugged at my beard—"you've got more hair."

"I've grown as a person," I said. "You get more hair when that happens."

Something rattled behind us. A squatty old man wearing a fishing hat and a dirty white T-shirt and baggy shorts was raising the corrugated metal doors of the arcade. This done, he vanished into the darkness within; shortly afterward rock-and-roll issued from the building, loud at first, then brought down to

the barely audible. Shortly thereafter we heard a clat-
ter as of crockery and pots and pans. We tidied up the
bench, crossed the boardwalk, and entered the cool
dimness of the arcade. Against the right-hand wall
was a row of Ski Ball lanes. The center of the place was
occupied by ranks of video games and strength
testers, fortune-telling machines and Whack-A-Mole
and transparent plastic cubes containing toy cranes
atop mounds of cheap prizes. On the left stood a food
service counter behind which the old man, hatless
now, bald with a fringe of white hair, was cleaning
things and cursing.

"How's it going?" I asked.

He scowled at us. "Won't be no food for 'nother
hour. Son-of-a-bitch kid didn't clean the fryers."

"It's okay," I said. "We're just looking around."

"Ain't got no change either," said the old man.
"Hafta go to the bank 'fore I can get ya any change."

At the back of the arcade were twenty, twenty-five
old pinball machines, their glassed-in faces decorated
with busty women in leopard-skin rags, busty women
in erotic spacewear, busty women in camo gear, mon-
sters, dragons, knights in space armor, busty women

in black vinyl assassin clothes. The machines had names like Galaxy Queen, Dominator, Mutate, Dark Destroyer, et al. The smell of oil and the mustiness, the thwack of the flippers, ocean light showing distant and clear as from the depth of a cave—it was the world I'd run away to when I was in junior high, spending all day in a similar refuge, sleeping on the beach until the cops would drag me home, and I was spooked by the feelings the place roused in me. Grouped in one corner were six machines whose names were written in a heavy metal-ish script composed of ideographs. Even the writing above the coin slot was rendered in this curious iconography, as were—I discovered—the numbers that registered the score. I fed a machine whose face was decorated with a magenta jellyfish creature holding gigantic spears in its tentacles; it was attacking a small but evil-looking black and gold spaceship. I launched a ball, watched it ping and bong its way down to bump against the flippers. I didn't try to save it, but let it be swallowed by the little hole.

I shot another ball and you said, "You're acting funny."

"Am not."

"You are." You massaged my shoulders. "You're thinking."

The ball became trapped in a circular depression with a spring designed to kick it back out; but the mechanism was too old, too feeble, and the ball merely humped up and down, registering points with every snap of the spring. I was going to win without even trying. Lucky at pinball, unlucky at . . .

"Try not to think," you said.

"I suppose you're not thinking."

"Nope." You gave your head a vigorous shake, as if to prove it empty of thought, the same way—I imagined—you might have denied some minor transgression when you were a little girl. "Only when I see *you* thinking."

"I can't stop," I said. "Nothing seems to help. Thoughtaholics Anonymous, chemical strategies. Only thing does any good . . ."

I allowed a dramatic pause; you arched an eyebrow.

"A kiss," I said. "That eases it some."

Your face softened, and you kissed me.

"You start yet?" I asked. "I'm still thinking."

You had another go. About fifteen seconds in, I decided this kiss should have a name, like a move named after a figure skater.

"Hey!" The old man glared at us from about fifteen feet away. His feet were spread wide, his arms held slightly out from his body, as if preparing to defend himself. "Don't want none a'that goin' on in here. Y'all gon' be doin' that, you can jus' take it out on the beach."

"Sorry." You kept your arms looped about my neck.

He continued to glare and said, "I ain't got no coin change, but I got dollar change. So ya'll can play golf if you want."

"Excuse me?" you said.

"Golf!" The old man pointed out a door in the rear wall, and beyond it, a flight of steps. "Two dollars a game each. You can tell me how many rounds you played after." He stumped off along the aisle, then looked back. "I know how 'bout long a round takes, so don't get no ideas."

On the roof of the arcade was a miniature golf course, poorly maintained but ambitious in design, incorporating several walk-through obstacles that were models of famous buildings, the tallest of these being the Eiffel Tower at hole number seven. From the railing at the edge of the roof, Piersall had the look of an isolated tropic—rooftops almost hidden among stands of palms, and a narrow fringe of beach curving off to the south. We selected balls and clubs from a stall beside the door and addressed the first hole, a dogleg right that required a deflection shot off the foot of a plastic King Kong crouched at the bottom of a plasterboard Empire State Building. Whenever a hole in one was made, an electronic track carried the big ape up to the radio tower, its eyes sparking.

The game we played that morning had a distinctly Victorian feel, such as one might associate with a game of croquet played upon a rolled lawn by a frock-coated gentleman and a lady wearing a high-collared blouse and a bustle. Our relationship encompasses a hint of role-playing, as do all relationships, but the extent to which we entered into our roles that morning was more than a little bizarre. We progressed from trivial conversation with the occasional touch of *double-entendre* to an approximation of courtly speech, and on the eleventh hole, which ran through a dilapidated twelve-foot-high replica of the Taj Mahal, its paint chipped and latticework cracked, this progression peaked. When your first ball struck a seam in the carpet and kicked into a corner of the Taj, we went to inspect your lie, and once inside, having a curiously antiquated sense of self, as if I were a penniless rake who had maneuvered the bishop's daughter into the shadows for low purpose, I kissed you and managed to undo the top button of your blouse. At this juncture, though a moment before you had been employing your tongue in a most unseemly fashion, you extricated yourself from my grasp and strode away, ruffled yet undefiled, leaving me to curse myself for having been born beneath your station. It was so pervasive and freakish a mental state, I later speculated that either we had shared a psychotic episode or else someone was beaming mind-control rays, tweaking our personalities toward their archetypes and making us better golfers. That, you see, was the strangest thing about it. From the first hole through the eleventh we interacted with one another like the Mountebank and the Lady, and were both well under par. But after the eleventh...I don't know, maybe they switched off the

Mento-Rays, because the role-playing stopped abruptly, and our athletic skills deteriorated to sub-normal levels. On the fourteenth, while trying to negotiate a looping course that ran through a luridly painted fiberglass replica of the Grand Canyon, I lost my ball in a rift in the canyon wall. You dumped your ball into the Colorado River and refused to retrieve it, the water being brownish and mired with plastic debris. That was it for golf. We settled on a bench on the edge of the roof and watched the stirring of densely packed fronds along the shore, kelp-like in their aimless rhythms, and the whitecaps rolling in, each dragging behind a train of turbulent water. You pointed at a shingle roof among the palms some hundred yards away and said, "Do you see the place with the gables? It's a guesthouse. With vacancies. I saw it last night when we were walking."

"You want to move again?"

"The TraveLodge is so awful!"

"We're going to wind up in a hammock on the beach. Ever done it in a hammock?"

"Look!" You nudged me in the ribs.

Small boats, maybe a dozen, were heading out from

the shore, each rowed by a single oarsman, moving abreast of one another toward the fog bank.

"What are they doing?" you asked.

"Racing? I don't know."

"They're not rowing very hard."

I peered at the rowers. "Maybe it's a fishing thing, maybe they're dragging a net."

"I don't see any lines," you said after a pause. "Somebody may have drowned and they're searching for the body."

The boats pushed into the fog in a more or less dead heat and were lost to sight. As I waited for them to reappear, I recalled what you had said earlier about us being older and beginning to know one another, and I thought that we had begun to act upon one another as well, to leave defensiveness behind and live in the day. With this in mind, I said, "Kay?" and when you turned to me, I asked, "What can we hope for? Is this going to do it for us?"

"I have to go back," you said. "But I don't want it to be over."

"Remember what happened last time you went back."

"It might happen again." You still had your score-card in hand, and you picked at a corner with a finger-nail as you looked out over the water. "But I don't want it to."

I stretched my legs and stiffened my back, sitting for a second or two like a propped-up corpse, getting the kinks out. I relaxed and my eyes took a quick tour of your body, lingering on your legs.

"Are you objectifying me?" you asked.

"As I might objectify the Pieta," I said. "Or Traci Lords."

The breeze died, and I could hear electronic bleats issuing from the arcade below. Apart from distant traffic noise, everything else was still and silent. Through a thinning in the clouds, the sun was a silvery, roughly cross-shaped blur. I felt that I was suspended in a moment just prior to some amazing occurrence, a blast of white light or a moon with Saturn rings appearing in the sky.

"I'll call," you said. "When you get back to New York, I'll call."

"Well," I said carefully. "That would be good."

An inch of time slipped past, and then you said,

"Do you want to talk?"

"It doesn't mean much to talk now...not if you're going back. But I would like to know if we're going to see each other again."

You knew me well enough to understand that I was asking for a commitment, and I knew you would not give it lightly, and the seconds that passed before you answered were charged with tension.

"Yes," you said. "I'll have to figure out how, but...I want to."

Your fingers tangled with mine, engaged in a gentle struggle, and then we kissed, and it seemed everything folded up around us and went away. I rested my chin on your shoulder. "The old guy's going to come yell at us," I said.

You rubbed your cheek against mine. "Maybe they'll never get the roads open."

"I think we have to hope for more than that," I said.

THOUGH NO DOCK OR PIER WAS ATTACHED to the property, there was a sign in front of the guesthouse that read TRAVELER'S LANDING, a somewhat characterless legend, I thought, to be written in such a florid Gothic script. The house itself was a two-and-a-half-story white frame structure with a screen porch facing the Gulf, a subtropical version of a New England bed and breakfast, run by Ed and Berry Malone, a tanned, leathery couple of late middle age. The downstairs was decorated in kitschy fashion. The upstairs, though furnished with secondhand stuff, still had a more homelike feel than the TraveLodge. We rented a room overlooking the water with a rickety queen-sized bed, a refrigerator, a mangy rust-colored sofa, a bookshelf full of well-thumbed paperback mysteries, and a balcony with a chaise longue. The bathroom was bug-free, and the sheets spring-fresh, and the paintings on the wall were Berry Malone originals, scenes of daily life in Piersall lent a certain surreality by Berry's difficulty with proportion and perspective. Palm trees towered to skyscraper heights, people rendered cartoonishly short and wide. I wondered if Berry might suffer from the same ophthalmological disorder as the artist who had done the distorted paintings in the Shangri La.

We stayed in bed all that afternoon, falling asleep at dusk, and when I waked I took a bottle of water and went to stand by the door that opened onto the balcony. Every light in town appeared to have been switched on, including the lights of the boardwalk, and even those of the closed-down rides. As a result I could see a fair distance out onto the water, though not quite to the fog bank. The whitecaps looked to be the same ones that had rolled in that morning, as if off in the fog someone with no appreciation of variety was operating a wave machine.

I got back into bed, and you pressed yourself against me and let me come inside. You were muddled from sleep, only passively involved, a drowsy animal capable of kissing and not much more, but as you came awake, you began talking to me, breathless talk, telling me how you liked it when I clamped both my hands to your ass and ground myself into you. The inside of your cunt felt molten, your skin feverish, and the rushed words you kissed into my mouth were like steam. You seemed so vital; I was a little awed. For a time I was more beholder than lover, like a doomed astronomer watching the sudden expansion of a star whose fire is about to wash over him. But then I was with you, part of your heat and you part of mine, and together we became a calm place in the midst of our own tumult, where every breath, every flicker of thought, every drop of sweat, every touch was speech. Looking at you afterward, as you sat up to take a drink, I became entranced by the soft pouches of muscle that supported your breasts and soon found myself observing in detail how you had changed. How all the tiny drags and failures of age had deepened your qualities and lent them radiant force. I couldn't understand how I had managed to live without you. The fact that I had succeeded in doing so for such a long time indicated less a triumph over fate than the ability to endure a harsh sentence.

"Jesus, you're beautiful," I said.

The bottle held to your lips, you said, "Thank you."

"You're more beautiful now than you were when we met."

"I wish!"

"You should believe it. I know whereof I speak."

You lay back down and pillowed your head on my shoulder. "Wouldn't it be fun to take a trip together? To Bahia...or London? Somewhere nice."

"You don't like Piersall, huh?"

My hand was resting on your thigh, and you caressed it.

"Oh, I suppose it has its charms," you said.

Those Cole Porterish, sophisticated rich girl lines you popped out with now and again, usually accompanied by a viper smile; they gonged me the way Tish speaking French always electrified Gomez Adams.

"Maybe we can . . . take a trip," I said.

"Maybe."

"Capri . . . you been to Capri?"

You said no with a sad look. "I'd love to go with you."

I told you about Capri, the little towns on the cliffs, the cool dim rooms where we would play. You listened with your eyes closed. I told you about the coves, the grottoes, the weird bar scenes, Eurotrash cobra women, rich American widows with glittering rings and sequined jackets and leathery tans, and I told you about the cottage I rented and the black dog who every night sat staring at my bedroom window with one glowing red eye. You captured my hand, brought it to your mouth and kissed it, then held it to your breast, and I thought I saw something dark and insubstantial swoop out from my forehead, following your movement, and vanish into my hand, becoming pale against your flesh. I felt in a Keatsian state of collapse. My spirit o'erthrown. O'erbourne. The city of my immortal soul in flames. I was down with the Romantics. Like them, I knew from experience that True Beauty proclaims itself. The eye of the beholder sees only its passage.

"Why London?" I asked.

But you were asleep.

I put on shorts and went out on the balcony. It was dark, and the lights of Piersall burned in carnival profusion, and the scent of the palms and that of the Gulf floated separate in the air, bitter grass and moon-aged salt. Thickheaded from sex, dumb with love, I stretched myself on the chaise lounge and looked out through the railing at the water. An apprehension shadowed me. I could see how we had proceeded from suspicion through the foolery of lust, and now had made a new beginning, one that would be harder than ever to pull back from because of who we had become. But once we were separated, the pressures of the marriage would exert their tidal influence. Things would start to drift. I resolved not to let them drift, to force a conclusion if the need arose. Several small boats, per-haps half a dozen, emerged from the fog and pressed in toward the beach. I wondered at them briefly and then tried to think of the various situations I might confront in the months ahead and how best to deal with them. They each demanded the same solution: I needed to close the distance between us.

Not too long after I had reached this conclusion, you came out onto the balcony, belting your white robe. You squeezed onto the chaise longue beside me, and I put my arm around you, smelled your hair. You laid your head on my shoulder. Within seconds, the rhythm of our breathing was the same, our heartbeats slow and steady. Lights like stars were scattered throughout the green town, and boats from the foggy west rode heavy swells in toward shore. The swaying of the palm fronds seemed to express a weary eloquence, like the wobbly feelers of ancient insect philosophers arguing in whis-pers over an abstruse point. I imagined the two of us tucked into a corner of this canvas, savage figures by Rousseau, shadows with burning eyes. We lay still as tigers waiting for game and said nothing—we had no reason for speech, both knowing all the other knew.

THE TRAVELER'S LANDING WAS OUR HOME.
Ed and Berry told us that while they were off at work,
if we needed anything from downstairs, some ice or an
extra towel, to feel free, and we felt free enough to
explore the house, peering into old cookie tins and
finding collections of fishing lures, buttons, keys,
sewing materials, snail shells, hard candy, political
buttons of recent vintage...there were dozens of such
tins. Dozens of everything. Berry's notion of interior
design was apparently influenced by the contents of a
Florida souvenir shop, a place that would sell blowfish
lamps and baby alligator-foot key chains. The walls
were busy with clocks framed in scallop shells, flat
plastic jaguars and the like, and the shelves were populated by photographs in mother-of-pearl frames, a
stuffed piranha, ceramic flamingoes, beer steins with
sunsets and palms in relief on their sides, every type of
tropical gewgaw. On a TV table beside Ed's chair stood
a framed, autographed photo of Maureen O'Hara that
was made out "To Eddie!" Ed's big moment with Maureen was the only item in the house we found that
spoke to either of our landlords having a past. No family photographs, nothing. Just a horrid collection of *au*

courant cheapness. But I could have lived there. I liked its cozy weirdness. You thought it was creepy, but were entranced by Berry's cupboard full of Barbie dolls.

Returning to our room, we made love and talked most of the day—there was scarcely any difference between these activities, because we were avoiding the future, and the past had dissolved into the present, and thus we talked a great deal about what we were feeling. You told me you loved me on several occasions. The way you said it once, half in a whisper, unsteadily, as if admitting to a shameful weakness… it unsettled me as much as it gladdened me. But that one instance aside, it was a glorious daylong life, easy and slow and sweet in every measure.

That afternoon I was on the sofa, leafing through a James Crumley mystery, when you came out of the shower and stood in the bathroom door drying your hair with a towel, then turbanning it about your head. You caught me watching and, still winding the head-dress, you said with amusement, "What?"

"Just looking."

You tucked the tip of the towel into the top of the turban and plucked your robe off the hook on the bathroom door and shrugged into it. You sat beside me and began rubbing moisturizer into your hands. "What're you reading?" you asked.

I showed you the book cover.

"Is it good?"

"So far."

Your hands done, you dabbed moisturizer onto your thighs. "I like it when you look at me."

"That's probably for the best," I said.

You rubbed more white stuff into your knees.

"Want me to help?" I asked.

"The place you'd try to apply it doesn't need any moisturizer."

"Is that right?"

"Yep!" You snuggled up and kissed me. "I'm in a constant state of arousal."

I kissed the inside of your wrist and slid my free hand beneath the robe to cup your breast. It, too, had been moisturized.

"I don't want to get sweaty," you said.

"Ever?"

You affected a plaintive look. "I was hoping for a half-hour."

But a few minutes later you slipped out of your robe and straddled me. Though busy fitting yourself to me, you managed to seem prim.

"Let me do the work," you said, "and we won't sweat."

You rested your hands lightly on my shoulders and worked your hips into a slow back-and-forth rocking…discrete, powerful movements. I started to engage you, but you put a hand to my cheek and told me to lie still. Amplified by restraint, the sensations became so acute they verged on the painful. Through slitted eyes, stupid as a beast, I watched your wobbly breasts, the muscles of your thighs tightening. Your turban came unraveled, the tip of the towel dangling into your eyes, and with an impatient gesture you tossed it aside. You braced your left hand on the back of the sofa and your movements grew less restrained. I could barely contain the impulse to grab hold of your waist. You let out a truncated cry, then your hips locked, grinding against me, as if you were trying to fuse our bodies, and I did grab hold and thrust into you, and we came together, in perfect union…though your peak lasted longer than mine. You endured a final shiver and collapsed half-atop me, scarcely sweating at all.

"Did you like that?" you asked.

"Oh, yeah," I said. "Very Kama Sutra."

"I bought a women's magazine in the airport. There was an article in it entitled 'Ten Treats for Your New Man.'"

"Which treat was this?"

"Six," you said cheerily.

"They should give it a cooler name than Six." I ran a hand along your back. "Can I get some Three later? Maybe a side of Four?"

"You're obviously not in shape for Three. A Nine, maybe. If you're good."

After you nodded off I lay thinking how strange it was that the woman with whom I had fallen in love was one who got sex tips from *Cosmo*, enjoyed doing window treatments, and sang me songs from old Rita Hayworth movies over the phone; who took sexy pictures of herself to send me, believed in NAFTA, and could change in an instant from modest nun to the Madonna of Hot Fun; who dressed in conservative, expensive clothes and looked like she had never stooped below the thirteenth floor. I had the idea that when I walked down a street with you in my usual disheveled pose, people would imagine I was holding you hostage. We had long since gone past being wary of our differences, understanding they were essential to the relationship, but their extent and range were nonetheless remarkable. Even the way our moods shifted were in opposition. I was pretty steady—I would get depressed, but mostly I kept it at arms' length—whereas your moods enshrouded you, your depressions enveloped you, often to the point that your emotions shut down. You once described your character as "phlegmatic," and I knew there was a passive cast to your personality, but I believed that a good bit of what you called "phlegmatic" could be attributed to a fifteen-year-long submersion in the despair engendered by a marriage you had been trying to distance yourself from since its inception. But none of that mattered. The differences between us, the person you were in your marriage, any other impediment or cause for anxiety—I didn't care about them. Watching you sleep, I felt I was standing guard over a treasure that could never be stolen from me, that was a part of who I would be from now on, and whatever came of us, whatever our hearts' result, if I couldn't sleep for a year, if every woman who passed reminded me of you and every ridiculous movie seemed a reflection of my life, if my health went to shit and my chest ached all the time, if I descended into a hell of my own making and my soul was corrupted by desire and thoughts of violence...I didn't care.

WE HAD BEEN IN PIERSALL longer than the desk clerk at the Shangri La had predicted and there was no end in sight—the roads remained closed and the phones lines were still down. That evening you went to the police department and tried to get a message out via radio. The police promised that the message would be sent as soon as possible, but their radio was out, too. I could tell you were upset, and I talked you into taking a walk along the beach, hoping the waves and salt air would work a change in your mood. I hoped it would change my mood as well—thinking about your husband had turned my saliva red and ropy. Darkness had fallen, and lamps in the windows of houses close to the water lighted our way. The sea lay flat, its lazy surges lapping the sand, and the breeze played fitfully, kicking bits of paper trash into the air. At first you went with arms folded, keeping your distance, gazing in distress at the Gulf. But before too long you brushed up against me, took my hand and said, "I'm sorry. I just didn't want..."

"I understand," I said, annoyed—I could feel a mention of your husband coming on.

"I didn't want him to worry," you said in a brittle tone.

"I don't need to hear it, okay?"

"I have to be able to say certain basic things. It's necessary to say his name once..."

"You run my name by him a lot, do you?"

"...to say his name once in a while," you went on. "Or to at least refer to him impersonally."

"Under the circumstances, 'him' is too damn personal for me."

You sighed. "I'm simply trying to explain."

"I don't need it explained! I can figure it out all by myself." I gestured wildly, in frustration, flinging up my arms. "This is my only time with you. This...from now until you leave."

"That's not true. I told you…"

"It's all I can count on," I said gruffly.

"I told you we'd see each other again!"

"You've told me a lot of things. You told me you were going to marry me. It was like, 'Hold on! I'll be right back!' So five years later I'm standing there saying, 'Gee, looks like Kay's running a little late!'"

You started to speak, but anger had hold of me and I wasn't listening. "I understand! A higher code of honor kicked in. You swore to be true to the son of a bitch who bullies you! Who twists your brains around every chance he gets! Jesus!" I stalked away and stood with my hands interlaced behind my neck, forcing my head down.

"You *don't* understand!" you said. "He's changed."

I couldn't look at you. "Yeah, right. 'Ever since you and me happened, he's pretty much toed the mark.' You wrote that in a letter, remember? He hasn't changed! He's the same manipulative bastard he always was. But now, you said it yourself—he toes the fucking mark!" I picked out a black region in the sky toward which I could direct my anger and shouted, "Fuck!" drawing the curse out into a bawl of rage. I spun about and said,

"What in the hell is wrong with me? I look in the mirror, I see a normal human being. But you…you have to see something else when you look at me. What is it? The impression of a REJECT stamp? Three sixes on my forehead? You need to tell me, because I can't see it. I know it's got to be something vile, but I just can't see it!"

"It's not you," you said after an interval.

"Then what is it? The Code of the West? You made a mistake, and now you have to live with it?"

"Believe me, it's not that simple."

"That's what I tell myself," I said. "I tell myself that all the time. But maybe it is that simple. Here it is the twenty-first century, and we're living in a goddamn Jane Austen novel. There's a woeful simplicity in that."

From out on the water came a splash, a fish jumping—not a loud sound, but it startled me, tuned my anger a notch lower.

"I know you love me," I said. "There were times, the last six years, I had serious doubts. But that's what they were: doubts. Because I was there with you, and I'm here with you now. And I *know* you love me. But I…" I felt myself starting to choke up and finished the sentence with a hopeless gesture.

A winded silence closed down around us; the action of the sea had the sound of something very big taking delicate sips. I came a half-dozen steps back toward you and we stared at each other for a beat. Two beats. I had spit out the body of my anger, but I was still bristling and unhappy, stranded in the place where anger had left me. Far from you.

"Let's go home," you said.

We set out again, walking separately. The sand sucked at our feet and a freshet of wind beat against us. The boardwalk came into sight around the bend, a neon skyline tattooed on the night. Red and green, blue and purple. All of the rides were running.

"I want to say one thing," you said. "About you and Morris, and why I . . ."

"I don't want to hear it!" I stalked away again. "I know more than I fucking want to! All right?"

"Are you determined to fight with me?" you asked. "Do you think fighting makes me more eager to be with you?"

You were standing with your arms folded, facing the water. A Norman Rockwell scene. The pretty wife watching the horizon for the ship bringing her man home. If I wanted to stay mad at you, I would have to start wearing a blindfold.

"I'm sorry," I said. "But I don't get it, y'know. Any of it. I can't figure it out."

"It's not your fault." The wind gusted, molding your skirt to your legs. "It's amazing we haven't fought more."

A horn of some kind brayed from the boardwalk, an alarm or the signal of someone's victory at a game of chance.

"I don't think about being with you constantly any-more," you said. "At least I thought I didn't. Now I realize I just didn't notice that I was." You aimed a forefinger at your right temple, gave it a tap. "Think-ing in secret."

I expected you to elaborate on this—to my mind—somewhat off-the-point topic, but you had no follow-up. You were schizing out, I thought, or maybe it was your way of telling me what your share of the pressure was like. Finally you said, "Why didn't you come to L.A. when I asked you to?"

"You mean the letter you sent a couple years ago?"

"Four years ago."

"Was it four? Jesus!" I hooked my thumbs in my pockets and moved closer to you. "I had so much going on. A book. The script. Financial stuff. When you wrote, it was like I overloaded. Like trains were coming at me from every direction. At least that's what I told myself. Maybe I blew it. Maybe I was scared of getting jacked up again and having it go to shit. I don't know. But when I saw you here, none of that mattered."

"Maybe…" you said, and stopped.

"Yeah?"

"I was going to say maybe it should have mattered. But that would be hypocritical. I could have walked away, but I wanted it. I'm glad it happened." A pause. "I hope you're glad."

I made a try for your hand, and after a token resistance, you surrendered it.

"Y'know how messed up this is?" I said. "When you asked me if I was glad, I wondered if saying I was would make it easier for you to leave. I don't want to think that way. I don't want to all the time be thinking strategically…decrypting your words like they were fucking code. I hate that!"

"It's not going to be easy, no matter what you say." You stared at your hand, the one I was holding, as if it were something that needed understanding. "I can't imagine what it'll be like when I get back."

"Truth be told," I said, "after about five minutes I forgot what it was like to be without you."

We embraced, put our heads together. "No more fighting," you said, and I said, "Deal."

You shuddered, a cross between a shiver and a hiccup, and hugged me more tightly.

"Are you crying?" I asked. "Don't cry."

"I don't know if I can find a way to be with you," you said in a weak voice. "But we will see each other again. I promise."

"Kay…"

"I want to be with you…so much sometimes!"

Whoever's fault it was in the beginning, whoever's fault it had been the last time, whoever's fault it was now, we were both buried under the same black rock of circumstance. I felt helpless, exhausted by the weight.

"That's why I have to hold back around you," you said.

I retreated to arms' length. "You've been holding back?"

You nodded, smiled, but your eyes were teary. "A little."

"God help me if the rest of you gets loose."

You laughed, and the laughter jogged loose a tear.

"Let's forget this shit for now," I said. "Can we do that?"

"I think so."

"Why don't we go to the boardwalk and play some dumb-ass games. Maybe I can win you a teddy bear."

"I couldn't take it home with me," you said gloomily.

"Then how about you win me one?"

UNTIL THAT NIGHT I had not seen more than six or seven people together at one time in Piersall. The town reminded me of an army base from which the troops had been shipped out, leaving behind a maintenance staff. But that night there must have been several thousand people on the boardwalk, playing games, enjoying the rides, gobbling corn dogs and fatburgers. They were pale and went about in groups and dressed in aggressively bad taste—lots of funny hats and loud prints and couples wearing the same T-shirts, bearing slogans such as Sexy Grandma and Sexy Grandpa. Rock-and-roll from the arcades contended with a tinny, circusy music from the Ferris wheel. We pushed through the crowd and stopped at a stall where you could win prizes by throwing darts at balloons. No luck there. Nor were we lucky at shooting baskets or ring toss. Giving up on the carnival games, we went into Joyland and found an unoccupied Ski Ball alley.

Few games are easier to master than Ski Ball. You roll a wooden ball down an alley some four feet in length, with an upward incline at the end and the ball flips up into one of five concentric rings. Fifty points for the smallest ring, ten for the largest. If you win, prize tickets are extruded from a slot beneath the ball return. First graders have been known to excel at Ski Ball, but the people trying their hand at the game in Joyland were utter incompetents. They appeared to have no conception of the mechanics necessary to roll a ball, and when they managed it, they did so either too hard or too slowly or at angle that caused the ball to land in the next alley over. I had been a Ski Ball junkie during my single-digit years, and when I started popping in fifty-pointers, a crowd gathered and applauded my every roll. For all the wonderment my scoring caused, I might have been Michael Jordan on his best night. The onlookers gasped and shook their heads—they couldn't believe it. They were watching a once in a lifetime miracle, they'd tell their kids they were there the night the big bearded guy shot the lights out at the Joyland, and the kids would laugh derisively, because nobody was that great.

Inspired by the crowd, I won hundreds of tickets. I took to showing off, rolling backwards, rolling two balls at once. Women shrieked; children gaped. When I made my way to the prize counter, people congratulated me and clapped me on the shoulder. I spotted Ed and Berry at the counter. Ed shook my hand and said, "That was quite a performance, son," and Berry asked, "Where did you ever learn to play like that?"

"I grew up in Daytona," I said. "Lots of heavy Ski Ball action." I asked where all these people had come from.

"This here's our busy weekend," said Ed, and Berry said, "Most of 'em's from Ohio. Chamber of Commerce worked out deals with a couple towns in Ohio. They just love comin' here."

"And we love havin' 'em!" Ed rubbed a thumb and forefinger together to signify cash money.

Even the old guy who managed the arcade—he was manning the prize counter—treated me with respect. "Damndest thing I ever seen!" he said. He waved at the shelves on the wall behind him. "Go on...grab what you want."

Burdened by a blue, five-foot-tall stuffed monkey, we went out onto the boardwalk and headed for the guesthouse. Word of my feats had apparently spread—people would point at us and whisper together. As we walked I watched pallid, flabby Buckeyes failing miserably at other games of skill. I had never spent much time in Ohio, but if these folks were a representative sample, the statistics on household accidents there must be off the scale. The shooting gallery was a place of peril; the Whack-A-Mole players had the hand-eye coordination of toddlers; the drivers of Dodge 'Em Cars spun in idiot circles and stalled against tires strapped to the railings. Three men attempting to play catch with a foam football would duck and hold up their hands to protect their heads whenever the ball was tossed to them. Perhaps the most startling example of physical ineptitude we encountered was the sight of two athletic-looking boys, ten or eleven, trying to ride a skateboard along the street where the guest house was situated—they couldn't even manage to stand atop the board, and it was apparent that neither of them had ridden before.

A block from the guesthouse was a bench facing the beach, and there we sat, you on my left, monkey on my right. After our experience on the boardwalk, I thought our little threesome would rank on the low end of abnormal by Piersall standards. Four boats were moving away from the beach toward the fog bank—I couldn't recall a time when I had not seen boats traveling in one direction or another. Together the stirring palm fronds and the waves made sounds like brushes on cymbals, and we could hear a frill of music from the Ferris wheel whenever the wind subsided. Your sneakers had collected some sandspurs—you bent down to pluck them off. The monkey slumped against me, leaned its soft dopey head on my shoulder. You examined the tips of your fingers to make sure they were free of spines and snuggled into me. It felt strange having you and the monkey in the same pose, so I slung an arm about your shoulders and shoved the monkey away. It toppled from the bench and fell facedown in the grass.

"Aw," you said. "You don't like him."

I caught a whiff of some flowering thing, a cloying sweetness like night-blooming cereus—as if the scent had been a cue for memory, we began talking about the past, good days and nights in New York, Madison, all our holy places.

"The night I realized I was in love with you," I said, "this night in Madison, a bunch of us were walking back from dinner, and I made a joke...I was teasing you about being tall, and you punched me on the arm. Affectionately. But it was like satori. I was looking at you one minute, seeing this great-looking woman who I liked. But no real emotional investment—none I was aware of. Then you hit me, and it's like I was fixated on your smile. The way you were smiling. Shy. Embarrassed. But pleased...as if you were happy to be playing around with me. I went back to my room and thought about your smile...about lots of stuff. Time I went to bed that night, I was gone."

"I'm sure I must have been there already," you said.

"There was a girl who liked to punch me in the fourth grade. Judy Bechtol. I think she had a thing for me, too."

You made a fist, planted it on the point of my jaw and said, "I was much more sophisticated in my approach than Judy Bechtol." You edged closer, and my arm slipped down to your waist. "I put a lot of work into it. Planning dinners and accidental meetings. I had to—you were so slow on the uptake!"

"I was. I admit it."

"Even when I told you I was going to dig a hole in your wall and crawl through it, you…"

"As I recall," I said, "we were sitting in the hall at the dorm with some other people from the conference…"

"That's no excuse! What did you think I meant?"

"Nobody'd had much sleep for days, so my first thought was I misheard you or else you'd scrambled the words. That didn't explain it, I figured you'd lost your mind."

We explored what might have happened had I responded to you on the night in question. The conversation began to depress me. We could talk about memories and trivialities and matters of deep emotional significance, but the conversational middle ground accessible to most people who have been intimate was beyond us, because we weren't free to bond in a way that would breed true familiarity and ease. I imagined how familiarity and ease would feel. I could almost inhabit the emotional space such a freedom would create, and I supposed that this might relate to what you had in mind when you said you were holding back.

Kids on bikes zipped along the street, shouting as they passed behind us. Insulting us, probably. But I couldn't make out what they said. A pent-up dog was going crazy in the middle distance; closer to hand, a swung-open door let out a gush of television racket.

"What say we chuck everything and go to Brazil?" I gave your shoulders a squeeze. "Catch the afternoon plane out of Miami."

"Okay," you said, playing along.

"Bahia...the afternoon plane to Bahia."

You tipped your head to the side, considering. "I'll want a nice apartment. A place with a tile roof and painted ironwork balconies."

"The old colonial quarter. Sure."

"And we'll have orchids on the ironwork."

"It'll be like Epiphyte World. Orchids everywhere."

"In the evening we can walk along the water and listen to the music," you said. "To those bands you told me about...the ones that play on the beach all night. And the pink church, I want to see that. And by day..." You fiddled with the seam of my trouser leg. "I think we should work some, if we're going to stay a while."

"I can work on a book."

"I've got a couple of papers..." You flashed a smile. "So much for work."

Light washed over the bench as a car turned onto the street and sighed past. Very softly, in a musical whisper, you said, "I want to make love with you."

"Here?" I asked.

"In Bahia," you said.

I didn't get your meaning.

"Story time...then bedtime."

"You want me to make up a story? Now?"

"Not like the ones in your letters," you said. "Those are too complicated. Like the ones you used to tell me in New York."

"I'm out of practice."

"Just a short one!"

"You want one about us making love ... in Bahia?"

"I think it should be appropriate to the moment,"
you said.

While I put a structure to what I intended to say, I
thought how strange it was that we always retreated
into fantasy, into the dream life we shared, even when
we were together. Yet the moments of that life had such
passionate intricacy, they conjured up their own reality, and I saw that this moment would be no different—a dream inside a reality, inside the fog, which was
itself a dream inside a reality, and on and on, an infin-
ity of Chinese boxes. I was beginning to grasp the fact
that this process was central to us, and to understand
that you enjoying stories and me wanting to tell them
was one signal of a larger process that both engaged
our differences and made them irrelevant: it seemed in
this and almost every regard, what you hoped a man
would wish of you, that was what I wished for.

"Ready?" I asked.

"Uh-huh!"

"It's eight-thirty in the morning," I said. "I'm

already up and gone. I've got a breakfast appointment with a Roman Catholic bishop and a high priestess of candomblé for an article about voodoo and politics and whatever else I feel like writing about. You've just finished showering, and you come into the kitchen wearing a towel and select a piece of mango from a plate of fruit in the refrigerator. It's cool in most of the apartment, because the sun's not high yet, but it's shining through the kitchen window. It's a high window with a low ledge and opens onto a partial balcony with an ironwork railing threaded with vines and white blossoms. Sunlight is painting the tiles on the floor beneath it. Alternating blue and yellow tiles. That's where you stand. You take a bite of the mango. The juice seems to effloresce on your tongue, and the sun... it feels so good on your skin! You drop the towel and let the sun dry the beads of water on your legs and belly. Thoughts slide through your mind like honey. But you're not altogether content. You're angry because of an argument we had last night. Angry's not the right word. Upset's more like it. You wanted to go out and play. I couldn't because I was working.'"

"Can I make a suggestion?" you asked.

"'Fraid not. My story," I said, and went on. "While you're sunning yourself, I'm heading back from breakfast. The priestess bailed on me, so I had a cup of coffee with the bishop and agreed to reschedule. I'm pissed, but it's no big deal. You're absorbed in drying your hair, and you don't hear me opening the door. When I enter the kitchen, coming from the relative darkness of the corridor, so much sunlight is flooding through the window, it looks as if the light's projecting your image. You're glowing inside it. The image of a lovely naked queen backed into the corner of a blue and yellow chessboard. You're standing in profile, nibbling on a chunk of mango. Its juice glistens on your lips. And your breast, the line of your hip and ass, they're blurred with golden-white radiance..."

"My *ass?*" you said. "That's not very romantic."

"I didn't say it right. Listen." I lowered my pitch to baritone. "You got a beautiful ass, baby."

"It's too big," you said.

"Your ass is beautiful! The whole picture's beautiful," I told you. "Seeing you that way, it stops me cold. If I was Catholic, I'd have the inclination to call the diocese and report a sighting. I watch you finish the mango, and then you glance over and give me a lazy smile. The sun's made you feel languid and hot, and you're glad to see me...though you've still got your grouch on.

"I walk up beside you and kiss the mole on your shoulder, just above the collarbone. You say, 'Hi,' and lean into me. I run a hand up your waist to enclose your right breast and give it a squeeze.

"'You've got a nerve,' you say.

"'You still mad at me?'

"You shrug. 'Not mad...'

"'Unhappy with me, then?'

"'Of course I'm unhappy.'

"My erection's poking your hip through the fabric of my slacks. You reach back and rub your palm along it, press it against my thigh.

"'This doesn't mean a thing,' you say, and turn your head to me so we can kiss.

"'I get caught up in my work,' I say after the kiss. 'So do you.'

"'Not like you! You're obsessed!'

"'Yeah, well...I'm not working now.'

"'Because now you don't want to work! Last night...'

"'How about I take the day off?'

"You hesitate, then say, 'All day? Tonight, too?'

"'Just let me finish a chapter first, okay?'

"You give me a cool look.

"'I'm kidding,' I say.

"'I don't want you to take the day off because you feel you're being neglectful.'

"'When I neglect you, I'm neglecting myself,' I say.

"'That's very adroit, Russell.'

"'I'm not bullshitting you. Last night was stupid. I was just erasing lines and then retyping them. If I'd gone out, I'd probably feel more like working today.'

"'I see. You want to spend the day with me because you're feeling impaired.'

"'You're going to make this difficult, aren't you?' I say. 'You're going to take me to task.'

"'There I was last night, throwing myself at you...all you did was grunt and tell me you'd be another minute.' You say this next with something of a pout. 'I'm losing the power to charm you.'

"I have a laugh at that. 'Now who's bullshitting?'

"You show me another lazy smile. 'I demand reparations.'

"'I think we can work something out,' I say.

"As I kiss away the droplets of shower water still clinging to your belly, you think my hair looks nice with a little gray, though it took you a while to get used to when you saw me in Piersall. But as my lips graze your thighs you concentrate on what's happening to your body, on the warmth pouring over you from the window. It's as if the sun has grown a tongue and is tasting you down there, flicks and caresses that send little washes of heat spreading from your…"

I broke off the story and asked, "What should I call it?"

"It?"

"Y'know…your hoochie."

You looked bemused. "What do *you* call it?"

"In casual company…pussy."

"I think I prefer 'cunt,'" you said after mulling over the choices. "D. H. Lawrence used the term very lovingly. Very appreciatively."

"Wow," I said. "Okay."

"Wait!" You leaned across me, grabbed the stuffed monkey by its foot and set it beside you. "I'm saving him. The dew's getting him wet."

"You might as well tell me your suggestion," I said. "Since we're having this break."

"That's all right. You've covered it."

You adjusted the monkey's limbs so it would remain upright. Its face was a grinning white oval, the features stitched on. Its head drooped, so that at a distance it might resemble a skinny blue child, somebody's passed-out twelve-year-old mutant.

"Where was I?" I asked.

"You were saying...about the sun growing a tongue..."

"I got it," I said. "Okay. Little washes of heat are spreading from your cunt, warming you all through. You stretch luxuriously, lean against the window frame and plant your right foot on the ledge to allow me better access. Across the way, a big dark-skinned woman on another balcony is hanging out her laundry. You don't worry about her seeing us, because in Bahia who cares about such things—you like that, you like the open sensuality of the place. Since you arrived, except for the days you were sick, you've been a little horny all the time. You think how much you love me. Not in words, not in images or memories.

You go to the place in your mind where there's a cell stained with my life, the place you call on when you need to feel me and I'm not around, and you summon me up, you let me loose inside you, and I start to fill you the way the warmth is filling you. Your thoughts are swirling. Thoughts about me, about what I'm doing. It comes to be too much, too much of everything, and you feel like you've floated out of yourself, as if your soul has gotten overheated—it needs a break, and so it drifts partway out of your body. You see pigeons on a wire. A samba has begun to play somewhere, blasting into the street. The dark-skinned woman on the balcony is dancing. Your eyes close, and the sun prints golden smudges on the backs of your lids. Something is changing inside you. Shifting, breaking loose. You know what it is...though you never recognize it right away. It's always such a surprise, bewildering and vast. A wave of heat and possibility that builds until you're afraid it'll grow too big, even bigger than you, and have to come bursting out.

"I'm doing something new. You're not sure exactly what. You focus on it, separate it from all the sensations engulfing you, and realize I've taken your clitoris between my lips and I'm worrying it, as if I were trying to melt a piece of hard candy. It's funny, you think. Sweet. You reach down to caress my hair. Russell, you want to say, and you hear your voice say something entirely different, a cry that seems to contain many names. You have to brace yourself on the ledge or else you'd fall...and then you're falling anyway. Everything that was dammed up has broken loose, and you, your soul, your center—it's overwhelmed, lost, tumbled away. Your stomach tightens and your hips convulse. You hear your voice again, soft and shaky and strained, like the release of a song that's gone unsung for so long, its instrument is creaky from disuse. There's music somewhere, a blue car passes in the street below, and on the tile roof of the *pharmacia* something yields up a dazzle. Love, you think. You think the word itself. The letters flame rosy in your mind's eye. Glowing in a pink fog that hides love's true shape, making it hard to believe in. But now it's taking up all the space in your head, and you can't disbelieve it, whatever it is. Nothing else exists. You want to tell me about it, but you can't speak, so you beam it at me. You aim it at my eyes and

beam it like a laser. Such communications are sometimes possible in dreams about Bahia.

"After that it's an unraveling, hot ribbons of sensation drawn out of your body, black rainbows in your
eyes. The wave that flooded you is ebbing, and you
imagine you're ebbing with it, going off wherever it
goes. Then I'm standing before you, my erection slipping between your legs, and you think how neat it is
we're almost the same height—all you have to do is to
hop onto your toes and I'm inside you. It's not so
strong as what you felt moments before, but you love
the feel of you and me combined. It's more exciting,
more personal. Knowing I'm part of you makes something not quite music switch on in your head, and
your hips catch a rhythm from all that extra sugar you
forgot you had, you've been keeping it secret for so
long. A white bird cuts the air above rooftops studded
with TV antennae, vanishes against the sun, which has
risen just high enough so it's shining in all our windows, and you make wishes...sexy wishes. Some for
me, for what you want me to feel. Others for yourself.
You wish you could feel my come inside you. Sometimes you almost think you can, and that thought

inspires you to reach back to the place where we're joined and hold me, letting my life throb out between your fingers. You hear me saying, 'God, I love you,' in a cracked voice, like the voice of a victim in the wreckage of a church, a shaft of sun slanting through shattered stained glass onto a tile floor in Bahia, and though you've always been uncertain about love, its nature, what it should mean, though you once sought to find a cure and still on occasion seek to disprove its conventions, you know with absolute certainty this morning what it means and see only what it proves in you."

I asked if you liked the story. You hummed a yes, pushed your face into the crook of my shoulder and said you loved me in a quiet voice, and placed a hand on my chest. It felt as if the elements of the story—the sunlight, the tiles, the freedom—were circulating around us in tiny fractions, dissolving from brightness into flecks of absence against the dark. We sat there a while without speaking and finally, obeying an impulse that did not rise to word or gesture, leaving the monkey—who suited neither of our purposes—to fate, we stood and went into the guesthouse.

I DIDN'T SLEEP MUCH THAT NIGHT, visited by anxiety dreams, and at first light I went for a walk away from the town, following the beach until I came to a dirt path that wound inland through a palm hammock and terminated on the shore of a narrow canal choked by hyacinths, patches of dark water showing here and there among the leaves and purplish blossoms. The canal was bordered by dense growths of palmettos and crossed by a little concrete bridge with rusted railings, no more than thirty feet in length. A tall sixtyish black man and a deeply tanned, thickset white man in his forties were fishing off the bridge. They both wore jeans, ragged short-sleeved shirts, and baseball caps, and they kept their eyes fixed on the spots where their lines vanished beneath the surface, talking all the while in lazy cracker voices.

"Thought we the only ones crazy 'nough to get up this early," the white guy said to me. "Don't tell me you after Baby Huey, too?"

"He got no pole, Fry," said the black guy in a smooth baritone.

"Hell, a couple ol' boys from the high school went in the water after Huey, didn't they?"

"They did," said the black guy. "But they was drunk. This man don't 'pear to be drunk."

"What you fishin' for?" I asked.

"Beats hell outta me," said Fry. "But he's a big 'un. Mus' go four, five hunnerd pound."

"Some kinda damn catfish, most likely," said the black guy. He had a lean, wolfish face and a pencil-line mustache sketched in above his lips. I pictured him forty years younger, his hair marcelled, wearing a gold lamé tux and singing doo-wop.

"Might be almost anything." Fry lifted his chin and scratched beneath it; the creases of his neck showed dead pale and tattoo-like against his reddish brown tan. He was jowly, with laugh-lines around his eyes—he looked like he enjoyed the beer-and-burger life. "Might be a goddamn gator."

"Don't water hyacinths take oxygen out of the water and kill off the fish?" I asked. "Even if a four-hundred-pounder could live down there, he wouldn't have shit to eat."

"You'd think that, wouldn't ya?" said the black guy.

"Antoine heah had him on his line," Fry said.

"Son of a bitch tore up my hands. That's how come I brung these along." Antoine kicked the bait bucket at his feet—beside it were a pair of heavy gauge work gloves.

Underneath the surface of the water, the hyacinth roots would be thick and there would be no room for anything the size of the fish Fry and Antoine were after. Baby Huey. But they were men of faith and I respected them for it. I looked down onto the hyacinths. A cloud of gnats distorted the air above one of the purple blooms.

"You know," I said, "I haven't had one mosquito bite since I been here."

"Hurricane killed 'em or somepin," said Fry. "We ain't had no skeeters since the hurricane."

"Crazy shit happenin' like that all the time 'round heah," said Antoine.

"You ain't fishin', what you doin' up?" Fry asked me.

"Just walking."

"You a nature boy, are ya?" Antoine gave his line a jiggle.

"Not really."

"Then you mus' got some trouble," said Fry.

"Love trouble," said Antoine. "He ain't fishin' and he ain't a nature boy, only thing send a young man out walkin' this early, he got himself some bad love trouble."

Love is a confessional emotion, breeding the desire to tell everyone you meet about its latest convulsion, and given the opportunity to have a hearing before two such impartial judges, I poured out our story. I estimate that it took close to an hour, fifteen minutes of which was given over to questions from the bench.

"Gotta get yo'self outta that mess," Antoine said when I had wrapped it up.

"You tellin' us the man knew how his wife felt 'bout ya," Fry said, "and he's drivin' her to a motel so she can meet up with ya?"

"Yeah," I said.

"Gotta get yo'self outta that mess *now!*" said Antoine.

"She mus' be one good-lookin' woman," Fry said. "A man ain't gon' act that whipped 'less the woman is fine!"

"I seen ugly women got the geechee eye can make a man do mos' anything," Antoine said.

"Fuck a buncha geechee eye bullshit!" Fry looked to me. "Yo' woman's fine, ain't she?"

I said that you were fine.

"Well, then you better listen to what ol' Antoine's got to say. Antoine's the man you wanta talk to, comes to women."

"I had my day with 'em." Antoine jiggled his line again and spat. "I believe I'm hooked on those damn plants!"

"*Had* your day!" Fry was incredulous. "Shit! Way I hear, you havin' yo' day right now with Lily Sanchez!"

I doubted I was going to receive any common sense genius from these two, but I liked their combination of sour affability and bubba enthusiasm.

"There the son of a bitch is," said Fry, pointing.

About forty feet from the bridge, the carpet of hyacinth leaves and blossoms was rippling, and plants were pulled down under the surface, as if something big were passing beneath, moving off to the south.

"Goddamn it," said Fry. "Look like he's tired of waitin' for us to catch him. He's done for the day."

"He be back tomorrow," said Antoine grimly.

"Time to start drinkin'." Fry bent to a Styrofoam

cooler and pried off the lid. The rippling passed into the distance.

"Gimme yo' eye, boy." Antoine turned his large and slightly jaundiced eyes on me. "Tell me what's yo' name."

I gave him a business-meeting stare and told him.

"Russell." Antoine said it a couple more times, ruminative, as if he were a connoisseur of names and was testing it for body. "You cain't let go this woman, can ya?"

"I let go of her for six years," I reminded him.

"You might not a'had yo' hand on her, but you didn't nevuh let her go." Antoine sucked his teeth, making a noise like a squeegee on a dry windshield. "If you ain't gon' let go, ain't but one thing you can do. You gotta make a steal."

"I don't know," I said. "Way she's talking now, we might have a chance."

"She evuh talk like that before? She evuh say she gon' leave her husband?"

"Yeah, but..."

"Did she leave?"

"No."

"Then you gotta make a steal. I ain't talkin' 'bout

kidnappin' the woman. What you gotta do is jus' put yo'self in the way of her. She loves ya like you say, she start seein' ya 'round on a reg'lar basis, she ain't gon' stay."

"What I tell ya?" said Fry. "Antoine's the man to talk to, you got woman trouble."

"Y'see," said Antoine, "she go back to California and gets with Mister Wrong, it ain't 'bout him holdin' her there. He's playin' her...from what you sayin', theah ain't no doubt. Man's lettin' her run, then reelin' her in. But that ain't yo' problem. This is 'bout her own damn self. 'Bout who she thinks she is. Thing you gotta get her to understan', she ain't who she thinks she is anymore. She ain't been the same woman since she fell for ya. Y'don't hafta do nothin' 'cept let her see ya. Don't hafta be tellin' her how much you love her all the time and sendin' flowers and shit like that. Fact, is, be a good idea you cut back on that shit. Jus' let her see ya and go on 'bout yo' business. She figger it out."

My opinion of Antoine's judgment was on the rise. "I should just go on out to L.A., huh?"

"You say she gon' call, wait for that phone call. When that call comes, do not delay. Get yo'self a flight.

Things might get worse 'fore they get better. But you got a shot, you jus' play it cool."

"How 'bout a beer?" Fry held out a frosty bottle of Miller Lite.

"Yeah, sure. What the hell." I unscrewed the cap and had a swallow. It tasted good and I said so.

"The Miller High Life!" said Fry, toasting the dead gray sky with his bottle.

"Miller taste like it got eggs in it," Antoine said. "That's how come I like it."

I finished the first beer and had another. Toward the bottom of the second bottle, because—I think—I was tired and stressed, I began to get a buzz and to feel more companionable.

"That your real name...Fry?" I asked.

"Naw, they gimme the name 'cause I like French fries."

"He won a contest," said Antoine. "Ate a whole mess of fries."

"How much you eat?" I asked.

Fry patted his belly. "More'n six pounds. Like to fuckin' kill me."

"Jesus! What'd you win?"

"Case of Blue Ribbon," said Fry.

"Wasn't Miller," said Antoine, "but it did the job."

I declined a third beer, said I had to head back. We shook hands all around and I wished them luck with Baby Huey. "We got a good feelin' for ya, Russell," said Fry. "You hang in theah now!"

As I walked along the beach I thought about the two men, and about Antoine's advice, which, though it accorded with my own inclinations, was less persuasive than their quest for Baby Huey. I had seen what appeared to be a large something passing beneath the water, but I did not believe a four hundred pound fish lived in the canal. Their circumstance—pursuing a creature whose existence was supported merely by a slight evidence of the senses, having little chance of ever landing the fish, and yet their lives informed by the pursuit—it was my own, and while this similarity was proof of nothing, it reassured me that in pursuing you, in loving you, I was not operating beyond the bounds of ordinary human behavior, a possibility that occurred from time to time.

At the guesthouse I found Ed pruning hibiscus

shrubs on the front lawn. I waved and he waggled his shears in response. An easel with an unfinished canvas on it stood beside the porch steps. One of Berry's distorted landscapes, depicting—as usual—gigantic palms, a couple of squatty humanoid figures, the ocean, and the fog bank. It appeared she was working on the fog bank, because there were a number of odd-looking lines in it that I assumed were a portion of her original charcoal sketch visible beneath a wash. I was about to turn away, when Ed came up and, with a degree of anxiety, pulled the drop cloth over the canvas. "Berry don't like people lookin' at her stuff 'til they's done," he said apologetically.

"Sorry," I said,

"No biggie. Berry got her own way of seeing things, and she does real well with her paintings. She's paranoid folks are gonna steal her style."

The notion that anyone would bother themselves to steal Berry's art seemed ludicrous; then I remembered the paintings at the Shangri La.

"Her style," I said. "The elongated palm tress and scrunched-up people. Is that something she came up with? Or is it due...is it just how she sees things?"

Ed looked perplexed, but he was opening his mouth to answer when Berry yelled at him from inside the house. "Gotta run," he said, and winked. "Boss don't 'low no lollygaggin'."

I climbed the stairs two at a time, not in a hurry, just to do it. You were buttoning your blouse when I entered the room, and you came over and gave me a hug. It was a gentle hug, almost maternal, and I thought something must have happened, you must have heard the roads were all right, or the phones, and were consoling me. But apparently it was simply your way of saying good morning with your clothes on—an aspect of domesticity that I hadn't experienced before. You began to poke around under the bed, hunting for your purse. I had a presentiment of how it would feel watching you hunt for your purse as you prepared to return to California. I swore I would be calm and resolute in the face of that moment. No train wreck heart attack psychotic breakdown this time around. I would focus on L.A. and the future.

"Can you take Denny's again?" you asked. "I need protein." Then, "You haven't eaten, have you?"

"I had a couple beers." I told you about Antoine and Fry.

"Are you drunk?"

"No . . . Christ! I had a couple beers."

You gave me an assessing look.

"We got to talking and they offered me a beer—it was the friendly thing to do."

"What did you talk about?"

"Mostly we talked about you and me," I said. "They gave me love advice . . . 'least Antoine did."

"Antoine?"

"This old black guy's got a Chuck Berry thing going."

"And you told him about us?"

"I don't think he'll spread it around."

"I'm not worried about that. What did he tell you?"

"Secret knowledge," I said. "Seven Sure Ways to Win at Love. I gotcha now."

You went back to hunting for your purse.

"You've never talked about us with anyone, did you?" I asked.

"No." You lifted a pillow from the sofa and peered in the crack behind the cushions.

"Not even your sisters?" I asked.

"They wouldn't be sympathetic—they like Morris."

"You told 'em what you've told me, they might not like him so much."

You groped beneath the sofa.

I pushed things around in my mind, decided not to pursue the subject. "I'm not sure what I would have done, I didn't have people to talk to. I might have gone over the edge."

"I'm glad you had somebody," you said.

You pounced on your purse, which had been hidden beneath a newspaper, and presented yourself as ready for breakfast, standing straight and true. I contemplated your carefully groomed, perfectly composed loveliness. The strength that had allowed you to be ripped apart and carry on without the solace of friend or confessor. The solemn curvature of your lips, the genuine mysteries of your eyes. I would not be able, I realized, to keep my promise to myself.

THE COUPLE WITH THE TODDLER was back at Denny's. I wondered about them. Where had they been heading? How had they spent these days of fog and splendor? They looked complacent, and why not?

Time wasn't their immediate enemy. They were a unit. They had a predictable future. The latest collapsible model that they carried about in a plastic case. They had weathered storms and sailed the sea of life undaunted. They had no secrets to conceal, nothing worth concealing, and I loathed them for it. Dad was about five-foot-eight of brown-haired game show loser, a sausage-eating mutt in his mid-thirties, growing dewlaps and a gut, dressed in shorts and a SIX FLAGS OVER GEORGIA T-shirt. Mom's face was sharper than his—a feral, lipstick-wearing, twitchy-eyed, drab little fox. She was church-on-Sunday pre-spinster mean and money smart. He was a Dork Junior College grad with an enviable collection of NFL memorabilia and deep concerns about the local building code in their hometown of Grub's Nest, Missouri. Their offspring, wearing a dark brown jumpsuit, resembled a chocolate truffle with hands and feet. They were so fucking low-rent-six-pack-family-values-porcelain-dog America, I had a mind to toast them with a glass of buttermilk and a handful of raw bacon.

"You look angry," you said, cutting your sausage patty.

"Just having bad thoughts about the world."

"Wha-at?" You kind of laughed the word.

"I was stereotyping our fellow strandees over there."

"Oh." You pointed at my plate. "Your pancakes will get cold."

I ate, chewed, observed. The three waitresses were playing cards at a back table, and I heard the cook laughing in the kitchen. The sharp-faced woman, mother of the truffle, was leaning across the table to the male unit—her tense attitude, the way her bony hand gripped the unoccupied chair beside her, made it plain that she was venting.

"Do you want to do anything?" you asked. "Or we could just go back home?"

"Maybe we've exhausted the joys of Piersall."

"I hope not." You smiled, looking up at me through your lashes, and nudged a scrap of sausage onto a wedge of toast.

The blueprint for a sinister plan to destroy your marriage popped into my mind. I filed it away against the day when I would go completely insane.

"We could have a picnic," you said. "On the beach."

"A picnic's good."

"Scuse me!"

It was the man from Grub's Nest. Seeing him up close added a dash of obsequiousness to my previous characterization. If he'd had a cap, he'd have been holding it down by his belt, crushing it in his two hands, shifting uncomfortably from one foot to the other.

"Sorry to bother you folks, but we saw y'all in heah other day. We figured you were"—he made a gliding gesture—"passing through, so to speak. Like us."

You were polite and assured him that such was the case. He had a beaten, plaintive look. Either he was doing some kind of shtick or else the little woman had had him fixed. I imagined the diatribe that had inspired him to come over: *Jesus Christ, Wally! Go ask 'em! For God's sake, they're not gonna hurt you!*

"Y'all heard anything 'bout the roads openin' up?" he asked.

"No," you said, and, with some anxiety, I asked, "You heard anything?"

"Naw, I sure haven't." He gave his head a shake, as if to suggest astonishment. "Y'evuh seen anything like this? I swear, this is the craziest situation I evuh been

133

in. Might as well be livin' in caves, gettin' cut off this way."

"Where you staying," I asked.

"TraveLodge. Folks over there, they real hospitable."

An opinion, I thought, likely based on free coffee, day-old donuts, and a two-minute conversation with the manager about the weather.

"We did a night at that ol' hotel on the water. The Shangri La?" said Grub's Nest. "They acted like my kid was, y'know, *The Omen* kid. I don't believe those folks been around any two-year-olds for a while."

As if responding to this mention, the truffle let out a wail, and mom shoved a bottle at him.

"Little feller's got some lungs!" Grub's Nest puffed up all papa-proud, as if he felt that having "some lungs" would do it for you in the world.

"The Shangri La *is* pretty staid," you said.

"Yeah, I guess," said Grub's Nest, apparently confused by your adjective. "But we figured the TraveLodge would be better for kids."

The werewoman he'd married was attempting to signal him, fluttering a scarf and baring her frightful smile. I pointed this out and he scuttled a few feet away, once again offering apology for his presence, heading back to: *You coulda asked 'em over, couldn't you? 'Leas' then I'd have somebody interestin' to talk to!*

"Hey!" I said, and he stopped. "You find anything to do in town?"

"Theah's a movie. Isn't nothin' good playin', though." He had an illumination, snapped his fingers. "You seen the gator?"

We allowed that we had not.

"They got a park straight in from heah four-five blocks. Gator's right in the middle. You can't miss him." He scratched behind his ear. "Y'all like donuts, they got a Krispy Kreme."

His mistress gave forth with a cry, a kind of vomited hiss—it might have been a name.

"Is the alligator worth seeing?" you asked.

"Under ordinary circumstances, maybe not. But it's got some interestin' features."

The truffle began to wave its arms and scream.

"Y'all have a good 'un." The man from Grub's Nest shuffled off to his little slice of heaven.

I felt guilty at having thought badly of the poor bastard. Then you made a comment remarkable in that it was the first thing I recalled you saying that sounded like something I might have said. Could we be growing together? Or was it simply that we both felt at such a remove from the rest of life, we had no kindness to spare it.

"That was like being in a *Simpsons* episode," you said.

THE PARK WAS A COUPLE OF SQUARE BLOCKS, dense with vegetation, essentially a palmetto grove with eucalyptus, hibiscus, shrimp plants and so forth interspersed. At its seaward end, a war memorial, a bronze plaque mounted on a stubby cement plinth, and at the center, an inoperative three-tiered plaster fountain with a basin of brownish water figured by archipelagos of greenish-white algae. Everything was overgrown, untended. The grass knee-high, the flowering weeds higher yet. The place reminded me of the scrap of Carolina jungle where we had walked the first time I visited you after New York, doing less walking than kissing. I'm not sure the memory played a part in our behavior that day, but we made slow progress in our search for the alligator, and paused often to fool around.

Near the center of the park stood a tall moss-hung live oak, and beneath its spreading boughs, in a rectangular pond enclosed by a fence of iron spears, was the alligator. It was a mature specimen, about eight feet from tip to tail, an oxidized green in hue, like verdigris, lying motionless in the scummy water with its back and eyes exposed. The beast had a festive look: Affixed to every visible inch of its scaly skin were hundreds of scraps of colored paper, each bearing a bit of writing. I say paper, but if it *was* paper, it must have been exceptionally stiff, because the water seemed to have had no effect upon any of the scraps, or upon the writing, which did not appear to be script or printing, but ideographs. From my vantage I couldn't determine how they had been affixed, but one thing was clear—you would have had to be very close to the alligator in order to stick the paper onto him, and this recognition conjured the image of people filing into the water to pin their papers to the thing.

We strolled about the pond, speculating on how and why the beast had been dressed in this fashion, but not seriously questioning the logic that governed its appearance—it was a minor anomaly in the larger anomaly of Piersall. The alligator never once moved.

"It must have eaten recently," you said.

"Looks about the way I feel after the Grand Slam breakfast."

I leaned against the oak, you leaned against me, and we kissed. Some of our best kissing has been done underneath trees. Druids in a past life.

"When will you be back in New York?" you asked.

"That depends on when we get out of here. I have another few days of digging around. Why?"

"I was wondering when it would be best to call."

"When I'm home I have to run out on business a lot—we better arrange a time before we leave."

"*If* we leave."

As we hung together against the oak, I thought of the time I'd been laid up with my back. You called almost every day, talked with me for hours, and were planning a visit. When your husband found out, the visit was cancelled, the phone calls dwindled and eventually stopped. You told me you were wracked by guilt. I knew you would call after Piersall, but I couldn't count on you being the same person you were at the moment.

You knuckled my forehead. "What are you doing in there?"

"Nothing worth mentioning," I said.

"Me, too."

"Bad things?"

"No, just...junk."

"Like what?"

"Like...you haven't told me if you're seeing anyone?"

The question put in a hitch in the smooth ride of my thoughts, and I had to think of the answer. "I was."

"Who is she?"

"This woman works for my publisher...in marketing. Anna Malloy."

"You broke up with her?"

"When I saw you at the Shangri La."

"Then you haven't told her."

"When did I have the time?"

You gazed at me soberly. I knew you were about to tell me that I shouldn't break up with Anna on your account, so I said, "It's no big deal. And I'm not going back to her. I don't enjoy making love to one woman and thinking about another."

"I know how that is." You drew me close, so I couldn't see your face, and said, "I'm sorry."

"For what?"

"I keep doing this to you."

"You haven't done anything yet," I said.

We were quiet for a while. A squirrel with a black tail sat up on its haunches beside the pond and gnawed at something. Jays squabbled in the crown of the oak.

"I have to say something," you said. "Please don't get angry."

"All right."

"I know you don't understand my marriage. I'm not sure I understand it myself. Sometimes I look at Morris and he's a complete stranger. Other times it's like we're joined at the hip."

I stopped myself from commenting on your imagery.

You continued on in the same vein until you reached your point: "I don't want you to count on anything from me."

"You think I'm counting on you?" I asked. "I'm not."

"You say you aren't, but I think you are."

We were at the brink of a conversation we'd had several times before, one that would be full of clichés about there being no sure bets, and how if you didn't gamble at all you weren't in the game, a blahblahblah argument that would piss us both off and leave you newly determined to make a go of it in California, and me haunting a Piersall bar, smoking cigarettes and swilling sour mash, feeling like a character in a bad noir movie, the antihero who must walk alone, the scar on his face testifying to the crime for which he will not be forgiven, the black star tattooed on his shoulder a souvenir of the woman he can't forget. It was amazing how quickly we had caught ourselves up to speed, re-inhabited our old postures. Yet somehow we had the sense to avoid the conversation that morning. Another instance of how, even apart, we had grown in the roles.

You laid your cheek on my shoulder. "I know we're supposed to be together...to have children. I know that..."

"Come on," I said. "Don't do this now."

"Okay."

You relaxed, let out a sighing breath. I closed my

eyes for a second, separating the feel of your body against mine from all the impressions that were flooding in—the push of your breasts, the plush swell of your belly, the firm volume of a thigh. Wind rustled the oak leaves, swayed the beards of Spanish moss descending from the boughs, and I had a whiff of creosote, a vivid streak of scent against the background smells of brine and foliage. The palmetto fronds lifted and waggled as if in vegetable ecstasy.

"It's beautiful here," you said.

As we made to leave I had the intuition that I could say something, that there was something to say, a sequence of words that would shatter with occult suddenness all our constraints. Yet while I could feel their shape, I couldn't isolate them from the clouds of less significant words swarming my thoughts. They were there, though—or if they never were, their shadow came before them. I put a hand to your cheek, traced your jawline with my fingers, and felt that same shape, the flow of the words I might have said, as if all life's secrets had for their source a signal we perceived to be a simple rhythm, present in every curve of light, every bend of grass, every gesture and caress. This apperception faded, and I was left to believe that I had wanted to tell you something less splendid yet no less true, a freshly comprehended reason for loving you— because you made me want to become the voice of a truth that circumscribed me, because only through the lens you provided could I discern this truth, because everything I hoped to say was embodied by the woman in my arms.

The alligator still had not moved, but the scraps of colored paper that had been attached to his skin were floating on the surface of the pond. Not a single one remained affixed. It was as if they had been held in place not by tacks or glue or tape or any other piece of hardware or adhesive substance, but rather by some incomprehensible force, and now either the measure of energy imparted to each scrap had been spent or else the generator that had produced it had been switched off.

I COULD NOT HAVE TOLD YOU THEN how many days we had spent in Piersall. It might have been all one day striped with nights, and those, too, blended one into the other. It seemed an interminable length of time, in terms of what we had learned and felt, and yet it felt like no time at all. It was the kind of day the early fabulists referred to when they spoke of "forever and a day," although we lacked a forever. It had appeared to be endless, but the end was near, and sensing this, we made love with soft deliberation, sealing each second in a vial of memory, so we might recall the deeper measure of the person we had come to know. The image of you I treasured had been replaced by a more vital image, the child-woman with whom I had been obsessed overshadowed by the woman of accomplishment whom I loved. We were stronger together than we had been, unencumbered of certain insecurities, our view less cluttered, connected on a more decisive level, and yet our basic problem, whether signified by your lack of will or my lack of worth, remained the same.

All that afternoon I explored the turns of your body, the deep country of your eyes, the soft occurrences of your breasts and thighs, the topography of your cunt, watching its outer lips blush and grow full, the inner pinkness deepening to a glistening coral, and your clitoris peeping from beneath its hood, obeying the chemical tides of our condition. For a long strand of time I lay motionless inside you, luxuriating in your feel, like hot oil on velvet, and then we moved slowly, almost stealthily, savoring every inch of liquid friction, every seasoned kiss, as if our prey, the entire world, would vanish should we proceed too quickly. We whispered simple words. Less than words, really. More the comforting growls animals make when settling beside their mates. And you, in your female poise, defining the space in which we lay with the richness of your acceptance. We talked, when we talked at all, of a future.

"I can get away in January," you said, as we lay side by side in the gray afternoon. "There's a conference in Chicago I was thinking of attending."

"January's a long ways off."

"Seven weeks. That's not so long. I can't get away any earlier because of the holidays."

"I thought he didn't let you celebrate Christmas... or has that changed?"

"We don't celebrate it at home. But we'll be visiting my family."

I studied the stippling on the ceiling.

"I thought you'd be happy," you said.

"I'm going to miss you."

"I'll miss you, too." And a breath later: "That's not all that's bothering you, is it?"

"Yeah, it is."

You propped yourself up on an elbow, looked down at me. "I wish I could promise more," you said. "I know you want more."

"What should I want?" I asked. "I mean what's the proper thing to want here? What's the book on the situation?"

You looked at me reproachfully.

"Seriously!" I said. "I'm trying to understand. What should I want...what should *we* want, two people in love with one another?"

"It's human nature to..." you began, but I broke in, saying, "Fuck human nature. I don't need an overview. I want to know about you and me."

"I don't know what I can tell you," you said. "You seem to think you know it all."

"See, I'm clear on what I want," I said, ignoring your comment. "I want to marry you! But I don't know if it's up to code...wanting that sort of thing."

Your stricken expression lapsed, replaced by one of confusion. "I had a thrill when you said that," you said, touching two fingers to your heart. "Right here."

"When I said what?"

"That you wanted to marry me," you said.

I had been trying to harden myself against you, to armor myself with doubt, and I felt wounded, my anger neutralized by the authenticity of your response.

"When you asked me to marry you back in Madison," you said, "I had the same reaction. It's so strange."

I thought to say that it wasn't strange at all, but it would have been a waste of words, a reinforcement of the difference we had never been able to overcome. Your heart beat rapidly, as if you had undergone a terrible fright or else were anticipating one.

You whispered something I didn't catch, and I asked you to repeat it. "I want to marry you," you said, and were about to go on, when I sealed your lips with a forefinger to prevent the word "but" from slipping out.

"Why don't you leave it at that for now," I said.

WE SLEPT, WE MADE LOVE, YOU SLEPT, and I lay beside you, my mind possessed by trivia, things I would have to do, calls I needed to make. Had I paid my cell phone bill? The people at *Natural History* and the editor at *Rolling Stone* with whom I had contracted for a piece on yet another Hollywood actor whose ego demanded he become a rock star on the side, they would likely be interested in hearing from me. I felt polluted by these concerns, that it verged on sacrilege to be aware of anything else except the problem at hand. All those commonplace matters seemed like bugs driven off by an intense heat that they sensed was soon to fade and now were seeking to reclaim their breeding ground.

A breeze pushed open the door to the balcony. Dusk was settling, and heat lightning showed through the fog. Several flashes in a row, and then a tremendous flash that appeared to illuminate fractures within the fog, a pattern of glowing reddish-orange lines like a spreading crack. The pattern seemed familiar. A short time later there was another tremendous flash, and I realized that the glowing fractures resembled the lines I'd seen in Berry's unfinished painting. I had one of those goose-walking-across-your-grave moments, the apprehension of something untoward, something too large to discern, like a shadow fallen across the whole of creation, and when you rolled over and smiled at me, I said, "This is a weird fucking place."

"Piersall?" You sat up, reached for a bottle of water. "Small towns usually have their share of eccentrics."

"It's weirder here than most, though."

"Maybe," you said without concern.

"Maybe," I said, "it's extremely weird." I reminded you of the clumsy Ohioans on the boardwalk.

"You're exaggerating."

"C'mon! You saw it! Even if I was...if I was exaggerating fifty percent. Even then it would be bizarre. That was like the Special Olympics out there."

"What's it all mean?" You said this with a blithe, almost British precision.

"Making sport of me again?" I asked.

"Evidently."

"Okay, what about this," I said.

I made a thin case for Piersall being a town populated by common folk and a number of imposters, the site of an alien incursion or perhaps a secret government experiment. As evidence I cited the peculiar fog, the town shielded from a hurricane, and the unanimous, unquestioning acceptance of this state of affairs; kids speaking in an unfamiliar language; the alien pinball machine; the clumsy people; Berry's paintings, which shared a strange fish-eyed perspective with the artwork in our rooms at the Shangri La; the incessant round trips into the fog made by the small boats; the alligator and the odd behavior of the scraps of paper attached to it; the derelict with similar scraps of paper affixed to his sleeve; the fractures of lightning and their duplication in Berry's unfinished painting; the miniature golf game...

"The golf game *was* weird," you said.

I had a thought. "What happened to us...y'know, getting all tripped out, then our coordination deteriorating. Maybe the same thing happened to the people on the boardwalk. They shut off the Mento-Ray machine, and everybody spazzed."

"Except for us—we were fine."

"We'd had the treatment already, so we were immune."

"You're being ridiculous!"

"How do you explain it, then?"

"Stress. Boredom."

"The people on the boardwalk were bored?"

"I'm referring to the golf game. We were fooling around and stress took it up a level. Then we got bored." You gave me a scolding look. "You don't actually believe our behavior was induced?"

"I'm just speculating."

"It's absurd."

"No, it's not. People are so accustomed to seeing what they think they see, they tend to demystify anything remarkable. God knows what's actually going on. We're trapped in a vast conspiracy all our lives, and we never have a clue even though it's happening right in front of us."

"I have a contrary view," you said.

"Gee, that's a shocker!"

"People are far more likely to mythologize the commonplace than to demystify the unexplained. Look at the tabloids. All the UFO sightings. The stains on garage doors that turn into the face of Jesus."

"Jesus does seem to be popping up a lot lately," I said. "But the impulse to see the remarkable in the commonplace, it could be a symptom of repression. We *know* something horrible is going on. We suspect we've been infiltrated, subdued without a struggle, our minds fogged—so we cast about for something that will explain a feeling we can't express."

"If that's how it is," you said, "I guess we're doomed."

A door slammed downstairs, either Ed or Berry leaving. We started to speak at the same time, and I said, "Go ahead."

"No, you."

"You know what we're really talking about here," I said.

"I suppose you mean," you said after brief reflection, "these opinions...we're defining ourselves with them."

"Yeah, what I'm saying, though, it used to mess us up when we had one of these conversations. We'd fight, we'd get stalled. Now we're playing with it. It's progress."

You screwed the cap on the water bottle, giving—it appeared—full attention to the task. "You used to confuse me. The way you'd bounce around from point to point when you talked, and yet it all seemed to hold together. I can follow you better now. Or perhaps you've learned to speak more coherently."

"Cheap shot," I said.

"It's not! I was just speculating."

"Well, I can see you more clearly, that's for sure. How your mind works. You got this one half of your brain that picks everything apart, and the other half...there's all this mist, and mountains and towers, and you're up in one of the towers dreaming about what's on the far side of the mountains, and here comes some guy, this minstrel or knight or somebody, and you're going, 'Hello! Up here!' and waving your scarf at him."

"So I'm half crazy..." you said.

"Yeah, but which half?"

"...Whereas your brain is totally diseased."

"It's a beautiful disease." I dragged you down to lie beside me. "It's the type of disease that wins contests."

I toyed with a feathering of hair beside your ear. "Y'know the idea for a story I sent you a long time ago...about a woman who begins to receive these exquisite gifts from some unknown person? Articles of clothing, jewelry."

"I remember...I liked it."

"You had a few suggestions. You sent me back this, y'know...like a document laying out all the permutations of events and possibilities. If Character X proceeds thusly, Character Y must be this way. I was stunned, man. I hadn't thought of any of the stuff you wrote. I got so bogged down trying to figure out which one of your ideas best applied, I never finished the story."

"I'm sorry," you said.

"You made up for it. You gave me the ending the other day."

"I did?" Happy, you gave "did" a second syllable. "Are you going to tell me?"

"It's too complicated. I'll show you when it's done. All I mentioned it for was to illustrate that we do our fishing in different ponds."

"This hillbilly imagery you've been spouting," you said. "And the fishing reference. I believe Antoine's been an influence on you."

"Antoine *and* Fry. They're beautiful, they changed my life. They should be on TV reading the news."

We became lazily involved for a bit and then you said, "Do you really see me that way? I'm in a tower, waving a scarf and offering a rescue opportunity for passersby?"

"Not like you're saying it," I told you. "I think you've been trying to rescue yourself for fifteen years, and you've gotten to like the guy who keeps riding back and forth underneath the tower."

The house creaked with a bluster of wind, but otherwise there were only the sounds we made, breath and the occasional complaint of a bedspring as we shifted.

"What were you going to tell me before?" I asked.

"I'll tell you later, all right?"

"Is it something I don't want to hear?"

"Un-unh. I'm just tired of talking." You cupped a hand and fitted it to the back of my head, gazing at me with mild concern, as if not entirely pleased by the effect.

"So it doesn't bother you the space invaders may have landed," I said. "Zombies from another dimension are stealing our rowboats."

"Nope." You smiled. "I honestly don't care."

"What about the alligator? The pieces of paper?"

"Don't care."

"The fog?"

"Ditto."

"The Sasquatch, the rain of frogs, the...."

"I don't care, don't care, don't care."

"Me, neither," I said. "But you know what?"

"No, what?"

"That just means you're in trouble."

You inched closer, the tips of your breasts grazing my chest, and rested your leg atop mine. Your dark brown eyes went down for miles. "I don't care," you said.

WHEN NEXT I LOOKED AT THE SKY, I had gone to the refrigerator for orange juice, and through the balcony door, I saw stars and a moon, almost full, out over the sea. Though I had been expecting a return to normal, this symptom of normalcy, so bright and oracular, struck a fear in me, sudden as a match striking in a darkened room. I looked to see if you had noticed the change in the sky. You were sitting up, submerged in shadow. My mind was clear, amazingly so, but the clarity was thin, endangered.

"Come to bed," you told me.

Lying there, harboring in you, I heard a humming in

my ears, some whisper of the blood that came like the singing of an electric religion along my nerves, converting me to the belief that while our bodies and our minds might travel separate paths, we were in some strange manner inseparable. Something like destiny was working itself out in us. Not a grand design, but a detail of a larger story that was at the least remarkable for its constancy. We seemed to touch the way spirits must, or clouds. Formless and interpenetrating.

"Russell," you said after a very long while.

"Mmm," I said.

"I'm thinking about leaving my marriage."

Those words sawed partway through the connection between us. I felt less adrift with you; the breeze was cool on my back.

"I've been thinking about it for some time." When I offered no response, you asked, "Aren't you going to say something?"

"I hope you do leave." I sat up, ran my hands through my hair and looked out the balcony door, trying to read the signs in the sky.

"I know I've said this before, and I'm not ready to leave yet, but..."

"Then why tell me now?" I said this more harshly than I had intended.

"Because I want to see you again."

"Chicago in January, right?"

You pressed your fingers against my forearm, then withdrew your hand, like a medical examiner testing for rigor. "I was hoping..." You faltered, and when you spoke again, your voice was stronger, more decisive. "You've always said you don't care where you work—you can live anywhere. I was hoping you could move closer to me."

"Closer?" I hadn't realized how tense I was until the tightness drained from my back. "How much closer?"

"Maybe California?"

Once you told me on the phone that you were leaving your husband. After you hung up, I set the phone down and passed out. It was a little like that now. I was lightheaded, and tiny flashbulbs went off in the corners of my vision.

"Russell?"

"I'm here," I said.

"You don't sound here."

I felt like man in a hurricane trying to hold his hat

158

on, everything flying off around him. "This afternoon," I said, "didn't you say...you said you couldn't
promise any more."

"I was still thinking about it."

"The rules...you keep changing them."

"I thought you were the free spirit, the flexible
one," you said, disappointed.

Mightily bewildered, I ran a few seconds off the
clock. "'Even the strong reed grows brittle in the win-
ter season.' David Carradine. *Kung Fu.*"

"Don't! I'm serious about this."

"California." I lay back down and faced you. "You
mean L.A.?"

"That would be good." You spoke so quietly I could
hear the pop of your lips when you sounded the B. "It
would help if you were there...if I left."

"And we'd see each other?"

"Of course...yes."

Shadow grayed your face, but I made out a worried
expression.

"Would you?" You touched my arm again, left your
fingers resting there.

"What?"

"Move to L.A.?"

"Didn't I say yes? Yes."

The agreement done, there followed a blank moment, one in which, I imagine, you were absorbing the blow to your conscience. For my part, I was stupefied. You began to tell me about L.A., the places you liked: a little Ecuadorian section, Olivera Street, a beautiful hotel in Santa Monica with a French name. I pictured myself walking with you there. You told me you weren't sure what would happen, you might cave in to the pressures that had always served to control you in the past. You never failed to warn me. You sometimes described yourself as "risk-averse." You talked about university life, the people you knew, colleagues and friends, characterizing them for me, as if they were people I would come to know, and though I enjoyed what you told me, though I was already putting myself in your life, living in that extraordinary yet ordinary future, I couldn't bridge the gulf that had opened between us when you said you were thinking about leaving your marriage. I wanted to bridge it. I wanted this badly. But memories of other such promising developments flocked my mental sky. Black birds with silver cataract eyes, settled onto the wires of my hopeful thoughts and plucked discords from them. You talked about the trees that bloomed purple every spring near your office building, the restaurants you ate in, about concerts and galleries, trips into the desert. You made it seem so attainable, yet in every word I heard the ring of a ruinous principle. It was not that I had misgivings about moving to L.A. I wanted to go there. But I distrusted the interval that would extend from the hour you left Piersall until the hour of my arrival at LAX. I distrusted not you, but time itself. I feared its elaborate dysfunctions.

"Russell?" you said after a silence.

"Kay," I said, making light of things.

Another silence, and you said, "It's Friday today, isn't it?"

"I think so ... yeah."

"I'll call you next Tuesday. At two o'clock your time. We can work things out."

"I'll be waiting."

Again there was a blank moment, and I believe we both were sensing the enormity of this step. It changed the sky around us from one of dull comforting shelter into a starry mystery that might abandon us, leave us for lost among its holy scatter of fire and ice. I could feel the fears in you, almost specifically, a tremor for every separate potential, and I'm sure you could feel my doubts, and there was still a distance between us, each half in our own world of hesitancy...until you abolished it. You trapped my left hand between your hands and pressed it to your cheek, and closed your eyes. "God!" you said in a voice that seemed to sum you up, hinting at terror and shame, contentment and delight. "I can't get enough of you."

LATER THAT NIGHT YOU GOT UP to fetch the juice. You took the carton from the refrigerator and remained standing there without drinking. I saw by the set of your shoulders that you were crying. I went to you and wrapped my arms around you and asked what was wrong. You shook your head, as if to suggest that tears were simple and without reason, explicable as rain, occurring whenever conditions were right. "I'll be all right," you said, dabbing at your cheeks. I thought you must have sighted a new and unconquerable difficulty ahead—I had too many obstacles in mind to want to know another. I said something reassuring.

The breeze picked up again, pushing the balcony door farther open, and the tip of a palm frond with dried vanes scraped against the glass. I saw that the boardwalk was dark, the clumsy tourists gone back to Toledo, Dayton, and the Rubber City.

"I don't know how I'm going to do this," you said once you had stopped crying.

Returning to L.A. or leaving me—I wondered which of these linked eventualities most distressed you.

You were still holding the juice; you had a drink and returned the carton to the refrigerator. Your mouth was tight, your eyes shadows. I knew you were starting to remember, or even to feel, how hard it had been to live the last time we parted. The freezer switched on, its hum vibrating a tray of glasses atop it. Out over the water, a wisp of cloud, no more substantial than a plume of cigarette smoke, crossed the face of the moon.

You stood close to me, your hands on my arms. "Are you going to be okay?"

"I'll survive," I said. "It won't be as long as last time."

"You didn't survive last time?" You were trying to make a joke, but it fell flat for both of us. "When can you come to L.A.?"

"I've got the tour to do. So . . . end of the first week in December, early second week."

"Three weeks," you said glumly; but then you smiled. "I can help you look for an apartment."

"I hate looking for apartments. I was thinking about using an agency."

"I'll drive you around. All over L.A. It'll be fun!"

"Yeah, that would be fun," I said. "When I get there, you know what the second thing I want to do is?"

You laughed happily. "What?"

"Go to Roscoe's for chicken and waffles."

"I could meet you there," you said. "After you do whatever it is you want to do first."

Neither the mention of fun or this byplay could dispel our gloom, our trepidation. Though the sky had cleared, we remained isolated in our own overcast. Yet there seemed to be something in the room with us. A distinct presence. Not Fate, but a lesser shade. The Ghost of Matrimonies Past, the Phantom of the Soap Opera . . . a voyeur, a souvenir hunter with a collection of semi-precious tears come to preside over the end of our time together, and to make sure we felt every instant sharply so it could fatten on our misery. It insinuated itself into our embrace, a slight gray figure encouraging us with vague pressures of its shapeless fingers to look upon the present as though it were the past. We had but one way to escape it.

Your face was full of strain, yet you went unhurriedly, the sensualist in you stepping in for the distraught lover, making me hard with your kisses, guiding me between your legs, and we stood by the sofa and made love. Once I was fully inside you, your hips rocked eagerly, and your breath came shallow, a dainty exertion, the way a cat breathes when it's mildly overheated. Your eyes were closed, but every so often you would open them and look at me, as if you'd lost track of what was happening and needed to find me to be certain. When I pulled you against me, you offered your mouth to be kissed, and when the feeling grew strong, you rested your forehead against mine—your breath shaky, almost sobbing. Sweetheart mouth, angel body, ghosted eyes...I wanted more, I wanted to be deeper in you, and I walked you backwards toward the sofa, taking baby steps so that we stayed joined; but when you sat atop the backrest, I slipped out. You took me in hand and made as though to fit me back inside, but instead rubbed the head of my erection against your clitoris.

"Is this all right?" you asked with an odd shyness.

You began teasing your lips with my cock, putting it inside you the slightest bit, then pressing it against your clitoris and rubbing with a circular motion. Yet making sure that we were connected mind-to-mind, eye-to-eye. What you were doing was not so much a usage, I realized, as a disclosure. You were shedding your last scrap of privacy, showing how you used me when I wasn't there, how you thought of me from time to time in the spotless solitudes of your ordered life. It was a perfect thing to see. Priceless to see. Nothing could have prepared me. You were admitting everything, to me and to yourself, becoming the wild young girl whom you had so rarely allowed yourself to be, demonstrating your license. When you were close you clutched my shoulder, lowered your head, concentrating on the feeling, and then you let me come inside. Your right foot hooked behind my knee, and your body moved restlessly, hips twisting and thighs straining, half-completed gestures, as if you were trying to escape a confine. And then a wave passed through you. Slow and heavy. I felt its belled shape, I swear. It must have been amazing for you, because what I felt of it through you was amazing in itself. Like an ocean swell passing beneath a ship. We both crested with it, and your arms went around my neck and you pulled my head down beside yours and told me things I could not help but understand in a language of pretty moans and sighs, sounding one moment like the confidences of angels, and the next like a woman exhausted by prayer.

BEFORE YOU FELL ASLEEP THAT NIGHT, you told me a story about your childhood. Our conversation had been aimless, far ranging—plans hatched, dreams of travel discussed, memories accessed. I can't remember what inspired you to tell the story or what theme it advanced, but it concerned a promise your father had made you—that if you did work in the garden, he would give you an Irish setter puppy. Apparently he hadn't expected you would live up to your end, because once you accomplished the work, he denied you the puppy, saying that a dog would be too much trouble. He gave you a kitten instead, and despite being disappointed, you had learned to love it. I thought the story had a fabulist importance in your life, being one of those lessons that manages to define our choices and devalue our hopes. Thus when it came to marriage, though you'd had the expectation of a puppy, a good young dog, you settled for a kitten, which had grown into a successful animal with claws, appetites, and, though it purred at appropriate times and slept curled in a chair beside you, a monumental unconcern for who you truly were. Of course you would likely consider this bullshit, and you might be right. But it was a convenient platform upon which I could build a hateful shape and so personify the debased form of luck that governed us.

I lay facing you as you slept, thinking how beautiful you were, and imagining all the strange calms and despondencies shifting through your dark head, the ghostly slides stained with chemicals that colored your light, and I wondered how it was I had come to lie beside you, what predilection central to those moods had caused you to move toward me. The sky paled to a pre-dawn blue. I recognized that from here on, everything would be part of the ending. I got up and went into the bathroom. In the mirror I saw a tightened mouth and haunted-looking eyes. I washed my face, dressed in jeans and a T-shirt, then came back into our room and sat on the sofa. You were still sleeping on your side, with one arm guarding your breasts. I found I couldn't look at you and think at the same time. Knowing I was about to lose you, even if only for three weeks, made me sad and crazy. I felt a reckless shape inside me, a gesture wicked as a scythe waiting for release, and my mind was active without purpose, seeking a function to perform, a thought to inhabit, and finding none suitable. I think I decided to leave because leaving was the only act that would serve my restlessness, my feeling that something needed doing and there was nothing more to do in Piersall except to suffer together. I stuffed clothes in my duffel bag, packed up my computer. I seemed to be watching myself move about the room as if I were a critic preparing his comments on a bad play and its tedious leading player, noting my "undead stiffness of gesture and apparent absence of facial control." Once I tripped over your tennis shoes and, afraid the noise had disturbed you, stood breathless and still like a burglar until I was sure you were asleep. I suppose I was committing a crime of sorts by not preparing you, but the impulse that started me on this road had been fleshed out with justification, and I knew that leaving was the thing to do.

I sat on the bed beside you and touched your shoulder. "Kay!"

You mumbled something, blinked. "What..." You swallowed. "What are you doing?"

You appeared to register that I was dressed; you rubbed your eyes and sat up. "The roads," you said. "They might not be open."

"Then I'll come back."

I reached for your hand and accidentally brushed your breast with the backs of my fingers. It would have been so easy to tumble back into bed, to make love and sleep till noon. But then you'd have to call California, and I'd have to hear it, and you'd be gearing up for guilt and marriage, and it would start to feel seamy and small-time on top of the way it felt now.

"You've got stuff to deal with," I said. "It'll be easier for us both if I'm not here."

"I don't want you to go!" You flung your arms about me. There was so much trouble in your face, all written so clearly, it was like a mask that might be hung above the stage of a playhouse devoted to the theater of loss. You kissed me openmouthed, your tongue flirting with mine, but that was sexual reflex, a confusion of physicality and intent, and not true to the moment.

"It's my turn," I said. "You left first the last time."

You nodded, your eyes closed. The sky was graying, the morning star low on the horizon.

"I love you," you said. "I love you."

I put a hand behind your neck, holding your head against mine, and said, "Don't worry about me. I'll be okay."

"I'll call," you said. "I'll call Tuesday."

"Two o'clock."

We kissed again, a long bargain-sealing kiss, and exchanged a flurry of "I love yous" and quicker kisses, withdrawing from each other in delicate stages. You tried to smile as I looked at you from the door and said, almost inaudibly, "Bye." You shed no tears, but tears were coming.

It felt unreal to go quietly down the stairs and out to my car—as if I were obeying a stage direction and my despair was the product of sense-memory, and soon we would be laughing together in our dressing room. I fumbled with my key and looked to the balcony. There you were in your white robe. You waved. I couldn't make out your expression but I knew it would be calm and grave, everything held in check. We were so practiced at this scene—though we had never done a balcony before. I raised my right hand and held it palm outward long enough to transmit whatever energies it contained, and you mimicked the gesture. The air between us seemed clearer than the air elsewhere. A salt wind stirred, and a dry seedpod clacked against a palm trunk amid a rustling of the fronds. I wanted the clouds to shriek, the green earth to belch fire, some chthonic reaction to this unnatural parting; but there was no such announcement. Life glided around us. With your image fixed in mind, I wrenched open the door, started the engine and drove away.

A few minutes from the guesthouse, my body was

so sick from not being able to touch you that I thought I would have to pull over. I floored the gas, trying to leave the feeling behind, and I was doing seventy by the time I crossed the city limits. But the road hooked inland through Florida jungle and there was still sufficient fog away from the coast to cause visibility problems. I slowed to twenty and drove leaning over the wheel and peering. I was thinking that maybe the roads *were* closed and I should turn back, when somebody ran at my car from the shoulder, waving their arms, signaling me to stop. Whoever it was wore a white jumpsuit, like those worn by biohazard workers, and also a mask—like a gas mask, only sleeker in design and a silvery gray in color. Or maybe it was not a mask. I couldn't say for certain. Spooked, I floored it again. In the rearview mirror I had a glimpse of several figures in white jumpsuits, and behind them in among the trees, a large shadowy lozenge-shaped object. It might have been a tank. The sort used to transport oil or natural gas.

Forty miles down the road I stopped at a roadside diner. I sat at the counter wondering what you were doing. The sunlight slanting across the Formica set up a buzzing in my ears. My face stung as if it had been slapped. Whatever our plans and intentions, I was once more in the place I most dreaded, cut off from you, having no way to learn your mind, alone and at the mercy of our luck. I ordered coffee to go and went back into the parking lot. It was bordered with Australian pines, and beyond lay an extensive marsh with tall grasses and blue waterways. An ibis poised one-legged in the shallows. Sun spatters spread across the light chop, so it appeared the bird was standing in liquefied diamonds. The sight of so much serenity brought tears to my eyes and charged me with adrenaline and rage. I threw my coffee at the trees, shouted, and began to kick the car door and then to pound the roof, causing dents that, when I noticed them, gave me satisfaction.

"What you goin' on about, buddy?"

Standing at my back, about fifteen feet away, was Mr. Assistant Manager Guy, a scrawny buzz-cut Marine wanna-be with an almost lipless mouth and squinty eyes and a narrow skull. He wore black jeans and a white shirt and an ugly tie. He stared at me as he might at an under-performing waitress. Meanly, disparagingly.

"Hell you cryin' for?" he asked.

He was perfect for my anger—I would give his body to the ibis. But all I said was, "Fuck off!"

"I ain't gon' have nobody goin' crazy in my lot," he said. "I can call the police, you want me to."

The urge to kill him had passed, and I wasn't ready to drive. "I got some woman trouble," I said. "I'm fine."

I'd expected him to leave, but this admission seemed to endear me to him. "Hey, I can relate," he said. "Few months back I broke up with my girl-friend—I like to tore up every bar in Fort Myers."

He seemed right proud of his achievement, and I guessed that the two of us could set right down and have us a brewski and share good buddy talk about the damage we had done in the name of love.

"Know what I'd do if I's you?" he asked.

Who knows, I thought, God might have sent this little squinch with His remedy.

"You get home," he said, "you just go to fuckin' every-thing that moves. Ain't no cure for being pussy-sick bet-ter'n more pussy. Hair of the fuckin' dog, dude!"

Pussy-sick, I thought. If only.

"I'm tellin' ya," said the guy, who could probably

count the number of women he'd been with on the fingers of Mickey Mouse's hand. "It'll do wonders for ya."

I wondered what he'd tell the waitresses. Would I
become a dangerous psycho he had scared away, or a
troubled soul to whom he had offered life-saving
counsel?

He tapped his brow with a forefinger. "Y'don't
wanna let it get in your head, man. Gets in your head,
it can kick your ass."

"No," I told him. "I wouldn't want that."

THE FOLLOWING AFTERNOON, I was sitting in a
Fort Myers bar with boarded-up windows, all the glass
having been shattered by the hurricane, when the man
from Grub's Nest entered and took a seat four stools to
my right. He spoke curtly to the barmaid and threw
crumpled bills onto the counter to pay for his shot-
and-a-beer. He tossed back the shot and sat with his
head down. He appeared to be muttering.

"Remember me?" I said, calling out for no other
reason than that speaking with him made me feel connected to you. "The Denny's in Piersall?"

He stared at me without a sign of recognition, then

turned back to his beer. I was in a rotten mood myself, and the idea that this fuckwit would blow me off after doing his Howdy Stranger skit for us back in Piersall... it wasn't acceptable.

"The Piersall Denny's, man!" I said. "The fog. Remember? You asked us if the roads were open."

Grub's Nest hopped off his stool and squared up with me from ten feet away. "Fuckin' drunk-ass motherfucker!" he said. "Leave me the fuck alone!"

The ferocity of his response bewildered me, but maybe I had interrupted him daydreaming about killing his wife. He glared at me for a couple of seconds, hitched up his shorts, and parked his mighty butt on the stool. He grinned at the barmaid as if expecting a hero's welcome, but all she did was stare at him fishily and take her hand off the telephone.

I suppose it's possible that Grub's Nest was in such a temper he didn't recognize me, or else he refused to... or maybe by driving out of Piersall at an unexpectedly early hour I had eluded the fate intended for me by the person who rushed at my car, waving me to stop. Maybe he and his pals had been about to introduce a memory-suppressing agent into the atmosphere, one that caused every human being in Piersall to forget all that happened during the fog. The tank and the biohazard suit add some credence to the notion, but there is little else to support it. Only the presumptive forgetfulness of the man from Grub's Nest and the fact that nearly three months have passed since I left Piersall, and I have not heard from you. This last is not a negligible piece of evidence. I can't imagine that you would have forgotten to call unless forgetfulness was forced upon you. But if the government or some other agency is experimenting on the citizens of Piersall, if the world is that relentless in its intricate foolery, I have no need to understand it. My half-baked hypothesis concerning the events of those days is—to my mind, at least—merely a conceit that allows me to remind you of our time together, of what we did and how we were and what we said to one another.

When you didn't call on our appointed Tuesday, I contacted your office and was told you were on break and had not checked in recently. While on tour, I tried to reach you several more times without success. I spent the holidays on various barstools in New York City—if I could have drawn a picture of my mental state, it would have resembled a biker emblem, a skull with flames lashing out through the eyeholes, representing not true anger but a hostile form of depression. Despair with teeth. I couldn't sleep, I shouted at friends, I broke up—none too gently—with Anna Malloy, I pissed away business opportunities, I threatened editors, I hated the sky. Whenever I was among a group of people I would grow impatient and leave the gathering and hurry home to be alone with my thoughts, preferring a depressed solitude with you at its center to the illusion of conviviality. My dreams were tapestries of violence and frustration, and I was tormented by reveries that left me jagged with insane configurations of desire. In hopes of restoring myself, I accepted an assignment that took me to Chiapas in Mexico for most of January, and there I gained a perspective and began to understand what must have happened. Often at night, whether lying in a jungle hammock or on a hotel bed, feeling imprisoned by your silence, I would conjure up your eyes as I did years before in China, and growing calm, seeing the dark shapes sliding through their depths, reading their design, I knew we were not yet done. On returning to New York I found that I had received eight calls from a 1-999 number, signifying the use of a phone card, all dialed during the week after New Years. You left no message—I suspected you thought Anna Malloy might pick them up—but I had little doubt as to who had made these calls.

I realize now that we have been found out, that either your husband tumbled to some behavioral cue or else you were provoked into a fit of defiant honesty, as has happened before, and told him about Piersall. And following that, traumatized, your gears frozen, wracked with guilt, subject to a passive-aggressive style of manipulation, you sat and watched our Tuesday pass, and went on to endure the anxious complacencies of the holidays. After six weeks, a length of time that approximates the period of your past recoveries, you tried to call, and when you received no response, you thought I had moved on. But I have not moved on—I don't suppose I ever will.

On returning to the States, my first impulse was to call you, but then I considered what we almost certainly would say. You would explain and I would forgive you. I would ask what all this meant for us, and you would say you didn't know. We would attempt to repair the damage and fill one another in on the previous six weeks, and we very likely would begin to grow easy with one another, to joke and tease and laugh. But in the end you would say you loved me in a voice that sounded as though everything in your chest was broken, and by this I would understand that love had once more become a problem, a deviation from what has always been expected of you, a chaotic element in the bland symmetry of your days. We have had a hundred such phone calls, and I see no purpose to having a hundred-and-one. Yet since I cannot let you go, since you cannot let me go, a response is required. And so within a week I will be arriving in California. At some point I intend to stand in front of your door and knock, and I will then learn the answers to my questions, and we will determine together if smog has properties in common with the fog, if Los Angeles is a country where we can live without regret, or if natural disasters are our only hope.

For now I'll send you this valentine. This complicated construction that has at its paper heart new memories, a painful history, and some simple questions of its own: Where are we going? What can we hope for? What should we want? Will you be mine?